FIC B CWEW

THE
WEDDING CAKE

Other books by Ludima Gus Burton:

The Love Potion
The Tycoon and the Schoolteacher
Only for a Year

THE
WEDDING CAKE

•

Ludima Gus Burton

AVALON BOOKS
NEW YORK

This book is dedicated to
Lisette Belisle and Sally Booth
who have been the wind under my wings from day one.

Prologue

The green leaves of the willow tree danced in the light breeze.

"I'm going to marry you when I grow up," Katherine said.

Her big brown eyes, shining with love and adoration, looked up at the blond, lanky teenager.

He ruffled her brown curls.

"Is that so, Half-pint?"

"My aunt told me to put a piece of her wedding cake under my pillow so I would dream of the man I'm going to marry. And I dreamed about you."

"Okay. In that case, I'll wait for you."

Chapter One

When the front door of the Pine View Library opened, a blast of cold air made Katherine Reese shiver. She glanced up and gasped.

It couldn't be.

But it was.

A smiling Andy Stratton strode to her desk, looking more handsome than he had years ago. Snowflakes melted into his dark blond hair and his fleece-lined denim jacket. Black jeans molded to his long, muscular legs. His blue eyes sparkled with good humor.

"Good morning, Katherine. It's been a long time," he said.

"Well, hello. I didn't know you were back in town," she said, relieved that her voice didn't wobble or otherwise betray the surge of emotion that flooded her. She

2

could count on one hand the times he'd returned to Pine View over the last fourteen years.

He dropped an armful of books in front of her. They tumbled and Katherine scrambled to keep them from falling to the floor.

"Mother said these are overdue."

"I'll check."

Her heart racing, Katherine stared at him from under her lashes. She kept her trembling hands in her lap. After all these years, his effect on her was potent.

"This is quite a snowstorm. I'd forgotten March in New York can hit us hard," he said.

"The snow won't last. Spring will be here before we know it."

Katherine piled the books on top of each other and shoved them aside, clearing the space in front of her. She fidgeted with a pen and laid it across the top of the pad she had been writing in before he entered.

"I'm here for Mother's birthday party. She'll be sixty-five," Andy said.

He leaned toward Katherine, his face inches away from hers. A whiff of his spicy after-shave drifted toward her. It tantalized her and made her very aware that this desirable male was close to her.

"You're coming, aren't you?"

"Wouldn't miss it," she said.

Andy nudged the pen and started it rolling toward her. A smile tugged at the corners of his mouth. He waited for her to react.

"Oh, you," she said and rescued the pen before it landed on the floor.

Andy laughed out loud, enjoying himself.

"Will you be staying for a long visit?"

"No, I'll be going back to Oregon. It's my second home now."

He headed for the door. "I've a list of errands to run. Catch you later."

Over his shoulder he added, "Mother wants you to put the overdue charge on her running bill. She made me promise not to pay it." He chuckled. "She must owe a fortune."

The cold air again reached Katherine before the door closed. He left her, unaware of the ache in her heart.

She closed her eyes and a deep sigh passed her lips. That eventful day many years ago was vivid in her memory.

Andy hadn't waited for her to grow up as he had said he would. In fact, he had married someone else.

Looking at their wedding picture in the local newspaper depressed her. Tragically, his wife and infant son died three years later. Andy continued to live in Oregon afterward. He was going back, and she had been foolish to let her hopes come alive on this trip. She should know better.

Still, she looked forward to seeing and talking to him at the birthday party. That much she'd have to treasure and to dream about later.

The next evening, Andy stood beside his mother. She blew out the candles on her cake.

"Happy Birthday, Mother, and many more of them." Andy kissed her and then turned to his dad. "She grows more beautiful every year, doesn't she?"

Katherine saw the brief flash of pain in Andy's eyes. She wondered if he was thinking of the beautiful wife he'd lost before they had a chance to live a lifetime together.

From a corner chair she watched Andy circulating around the crowded room, talking and laughing with everyone.

His blond hair was thick, with a tendency to wave. He still kept it cut short. Tonight he had pushed up the sleeves of his black turtleneck to reveal hard muscles. His broad shoulders, which had helped him to barrel into the other team in football, looked as muscular and strong as ever. Without a doubt, Andy Stratton had only gotten better looking with the years.

He made her heartbeat quicken as always.

Later, as she prepared to leave the party, Katherine said to Mrs. Stratton, "I hope you have many more birthdays for us to celebrate."

"The way I feel tonight, I shall go on and on," Andy's mother said with a hearty laugh. "The best part was having Andy here. I wish he would move back to Pine View. He's determined to stay in Oregon, however."

"After my Dad died," Katherine said, "I was fortunate to get the librarian job here and keep my mother company. I'll be content to live in Pine View for the rest of my life."

"I hope you aren't going to be only a career woman. You should get married and have children too."

"I agree with you," Katherine said, "but I have to find the right man first."

Andy's mother moved closer to her and said in a low voice, "You don't have to look far away. I think I know the one for you." She raised her eyebrows and nodded toward Andy.

Katherine felt the blush dyeing her cheeks. She quickly said, "Please, don't say anything like that to Andy. He's never shown any interest in me."

Mrs. Stratton gave a small smile. "We'll wait and see."

"Good night," Katherine said and walked quickly toward the door.

Andy blocked her way. "Not leaving already? I haven't had a chance to talk to you."

His gaze swept over her. Her heart-shaped face, dark brown eyes curtained by long, curled lashes and sensuous mouth caused his breath to become shallow.

"You don't look anything like the tomboy who used to follow me around."

"I've grown up," she said. She felt a blush move across her cheeks.

"You certainly have. I like the change."

"Thank you."

Before she could move past him, he reached up and removed the pins from her hair. He laughed at her surprise.

"You shouldn't wear your hair in a bun." Her curls fell down her back at his touch. "There, that's better."

6

"Oh," Katherine gasped. Then she laughed. "Andy, you never change."

His next words left her speechless.

"You're a beautiful woman, Katherine. You shouldn't hide behind those high collars and hair pulled back so tightly."

She had always considered her looks as ordinary. Dating Franklin Perry, the local banker, raised her self-esteem, but he hadn't showered her with compliments about her beauty. She shook her head. She wasn't going to be swayed by Andy's compliments. He was just being kind.

"I have to leave," she said and took a step toward the door.

He stepped aside to let her go.

"I hope we can talk another time. I'm glad you came to make Mother's party a success."

He opened the door. "Good night, Katherine."

Katherine slipped out and crossed their adjoining backyards almost at a run. She stepped into her house and leaned against the closed door.

She kept hearing Andy's words, "You're a beautiful woman, Katherine."

If only she could believe him.

At 9:00 in the morning, two days after the birthday party, Katherine walked to the post office where everyone picked up his mail. She carried her grandmother's old basket over her arm. The library mail filled it today.

A green bow on the basket's handle reminded her to finish decorating the library for St. Patrick's Day.

"What's with the basket?" Andy came up behind her.

As though on cue, her heart began to race, and she took in a big gulp of air. She turned around and smiled at him. His devastating, answering smile was like a warm sunbeam radiating heat all over her.

"It's my mail basket," she said. "What a surprise to see you. I thought you had gone back to Oregon."

"I decided to stay longer and get reacquainted with the village. I'm seeing it—and you—in a new light," Andy said. "Let me carry that basket."

She hoped he'd never know how much those two words disturbed her peace of mind and caused delight to surge through her being. Without a word of protest, she gave the basket to him. In spite of its weight, he swung it back and forth.

"Thank you," she managed to say in a firm voice. "Most of the library's mail comes on Monday. "I appreciate the help."

"I always want to be a help to you." His answer was soft, caressing the "you."

If Andy continued to say such disturbing things, Katherine didn't know if she could hide her feelings from him. She looked straight ahead of her. He was just being . . . well, Andy.

They walked in companionable silence toward the library. Katherine noticed that Andy was looking closely at every business on the street, almost as though he had never seen the hardware store or the supermarket before. When they came to Pine's Restaurant, which was next to the library, he asked, "How about having a cup of coffee with me?"

"I can't. The library opens in a few minutes."

Still holding the basket, Andy walked her to the door of the library. He looked up and down the length of Main Street and then out beyond the village limits. The library was the last building on that side of the street. While she unlocked the door, he spoke, more to himself than to her.

"Every lot within the village limits contains a business. The only vacant space is on the other side of the library."

"True," Katherine agreed. She didn't tell Andy that the spot would soon have the future addition to the library.

While he gazed out of the village limits he continued talking in the same thoughtful vein, "The Pine View Central School has the acreage on the other side of the highway. What about the land across from the school?"

"Can't build there. Most of the land along the highway is federally protected wetlands. There may be acres in back of them that are okay," Katherine said. "Why are you so interested in all this?"

"Just trying to sort out some things in my mind." Andy handed her the basket of mail. "Have to get going. I'd like to come in and talk, but I need to check on some things before I leave for Oregon at five."

While Katherine unlocked the door, she wondered how long it would be before he came back. Though he had shown no special interest in her on this visit, her old feelings had come alive. Did she really fall in love with Andy when she was only twelve years old? Whatever the feeling, it wouldn't go away.

She turned around to look at him for the last time. "Good-bye and have a safe trip."

"Bye, Half-pint."

Astonishment rooted her to the spot. She watched Andy walk down the street until he turned on to Bridge Street.

Oh, my!

Andy had called her Half-pint, his name for her when she was twelve, and he was a tall sixteen. This much he remembered of the past. Only she remembered that she put the wedding cake under her pillow and dreamed about marrying him. After that day, she had foolishly hoped he'd wait for her to grow up. But he hadn't. She kept reminding herself that he married someone else.

Katherine gave a short laugh. She needed to forget the past. Stacks of books awaited her. Andy was gone, and she refused to think about him. She had done it before. Only it would be much harder to do now.

Seeing him again ignited the desires she had been pushing aside. She wanted love, marriage, and a family. She knew what kind of a marriage she had to have. She wanted her heart to leap with joy when her man entered the room. To run into his arms and be kissed breathless. To live the rest of her life with him.

Andy.

No! She wasn't going to think about Andy. Touching

her hair at the party and calling her by a casual nickname didn't make a marriage. Besides, he was going to live a continent away from her. At the rate she was going, if she couldn't have Andy, she might have to leave Pine View to find a man who met her expectations.

Before she made such a radical change in her life, she would leave a legacy behind her—an addition to the library on the adjoining lot. The lovely old Victorian house that had served as the town's library for twenty-five years was filled to capacity. They needed space for a section on local history and an expansion of the children's department.

She felt sure she could get a federal grant to pay for the building. The village board had been receptive to this plan the last time she met with them. The townspeople would vote on it at the next monthly meeting.

While she had been sitting idly at her desk, the pile of books to be checked in and put on the shelves didn't move by themselves. Before she reached for the books, the front door slammed against the brass doorstop. The sound reverberated loudly. Franklin Perry entered.

"What's the matter? You never leave the bank at this hour."

"Where's Andy?" Franklin's gaze swept around the library.

"Andy? I assume he's at his house getting ready to return to Oregon this afternoon," Katherine said, keeping her voice casual. "Why do you think he's here?"

"I saw him walking with you and carrying your basket."

"So?"

"I . . . I . . . guess I jumped to the wrong conclusion."

"And what was that?" Katherine's eyebrows rose.

"I thought he would ask you out tonight."

"Really? How ridiculous. Andy isn't even going to be in town after today. He came for his mother's birthday. I was glad to have his help carrying my mail." She pushed aside the pile of books. "Is there anything else you want?"

Franklin pulled the knot of his tie tighter. "Will you have dinner with me tonight?"

"No, sorry, but I have other plans."

"I'd really like to take you out," Franklin persisted.

"Later in the week would be better for me." Katherine added, "I'm sorry to cut this short, but I must get to work."

"I'll call you later," Franklin said before he opened the door.

Katherine smiled and nodded her head. "Good-bye, Franklin."

After he left, Katherine laughed. Franklin's reaction to Andy surprised her until she remembered that they had been rivals in every way in high school. How different the two men were. Franklin, with dark hair and eyes, was quiet, intense, and ambitious. Andy was tall and blond, endowed with charm, and had an easy-going attitude that made him popular with everyone.

She put all thoughts of both Andy and Franklin behind her and worked on her proposal to the village board for the addition. Though only a formality, it needed to be put on paper. Although the building would require tax money for its upkeep, she didn't expect any opposition. Very few neighboring villages had as fine a library as Pine View's.

According to her plans, the library addition would look like a wing of the present house, in keeping with the preservation society's code. As president of the society for a third term, she took pride in her accomplishments. The Victorian look of Main Street was much admired by tourists and residents. They often expressed their approval and liked the feeling of taking a step back to a more peaceful and beautiful past.

She smiled, thinking of some of the early battles she and the other ladies had waged with the shop owners in order to accomplish this feat. With only her addition to fill in the last space, the entire length of Main Street would be Victorian in design.

She suddenly remembered Andy's comments about the village and Main Street.

What was he thinking?

Chapter Two

In Oregon, Andy Stratton spent a hectic three weeks negotiating the final details for the purchase of a small computer chip manufacturing company. He had worked for Jonas Whitner for six years. Jonas, having no family to pass on his company to, had decided to sell the business and retire. Because he liked and admired Andy, he made reasonable arrangements for him to buy the company.

"What's this? You're not going to stay here?" This news startled Jonas. "I thought you'd continue doing business in Portland."

"I'm going home," Andy said. "I didn't realize how much I wanted to be there until I went back. Mom is sixty-five and my dad is seventy. I need to be close to them instead of having a continent between us."

"Where will you relocate?" Jonas asked.

14

"I want to build the business in the village."

"Tell me about your plans."

Andy expounded on his ideas, especially the need to have his company in the village so his employees could walk to work if they wanted to do so.

"Sounds good to me. No one likes the hassle of driving to work every day." Jonas shook Andy's hand. "I wish you all the luck in the world. Let me know how things work out."

"Sure thing. I'll keep in touch. I'd never have gotten through these four years after Allison died without you," Andy said.

"My pleasure, son. I'll see you at the lawyer's office."

Andy walked to his car and got in. He sat there, thinking about the big change he was making in his life. After he and Allison married, he thought the area around Portland would be his permanent home.

Allison, his darling wife.

Without warning, his last minutes with her came flooding back. His breath caught in his throat and tears ran down his cheeks. The pain of his loss was as poignant today as the day it happened.

He had just returned from the nurse's station.

From the doorway he looked at his wife as she lay in the hospital bed. The dark shadows under her closed eyes made her cheeks appear whiter than ever. Her black, curly hair framed her face and fanned out on the white pillow. She looked like a porcelain doll.

Terror struck his heart. Was Allison still alive? She had to be. He couldn't lose her. He walked quickly to the bed.

Looking down on her, guilt gripped him. Since he knew she wasn't strong, he should have protected her, should never have gotten her pregnant. It didn't matter that she desperately desired to have his baby. Why hadn't he listened to his instincts? He hadn't, and now it was his fault she was dying.

Then, slowly, her eyelids opened. She saw him and a sweet smile of welcome curved her pale lips.

He sank to his knees by the bed. Taking her hand gently in both of his, he tried to hold her to him in this life. He bent over, and his kiss was feather-light.

"I'm so glad you're here," she murmured. "Please do something for me."

"Anything. You know that, my darling."

Again came her smile, and her gaze filled with love for him.

"You've made me very happy since the first moment we met," she said in a whisper. "But things change. I have to leave you—"

"No! No! Don't even think it."

She shook her head slowly. "I want you to promise that you will go on and find someone to be a mother to our precious son and to fill your life, as well."

Her fingers clutched tighter around his hand.

"Promise me."

Andy laid his forehead on their hands. How could he bear this? No one would ever fill his heart and life as she had done. She was asking—and he couldn't refuse her.

16

"I promise, I promise," he said, the words being torn from his heart.

A soft sigh passed through her lips. "I love you," she said. She gave him another love-filled smile. Her eyes drifted shut and her spirit slipped away from him.

As her fingers relaxed around his, he knew that she was gone.

Andy had no memory of the next minutes and hours. All he remembered was feeling like his world had come to an end.

Three days later, his beloved son, the proof of their love, also died. More guilt descended on him. The two most important people in his life had died because of him. His agony was complete, and he would never be able to forgive himself.

He didn't know how he continued living. He wanted to die and be with them. But life went on. He hid his guilty feelings and told no one about them.

He buried Allison and his infant son Jeffrey in her family cemetery plot outside Portland. Each week he took flowers to place before the simple stone that read:

ALLISON GRAY STRATTON, BELOVED WIFE
JEFFREY GORDON STRATTON, BELOVED SON

The date was forever engraved in his memory. He didn't need to read it on the marker.

* * *

It took Andy several minutes before he put aside his memories. He started the car and drove to his apartment.

Having sold their little house, he had no real estate ties in Oregon. When he moved to Pine View, he could no longer go to the grass-covered plot. This was the hardest thing he had to do. However, Allison and his son would always be with him in his heart.

He was making the right decision to locate his new company in Pine View. He'd like to start building by June 1, and be manufacturing computer chips by September 1. Maybe he was being too optimistic, but there was nothing like a deadline to keep him moving forward.

Plans for his future filled Andy's thoughts. He would first break the news to his parents. Thinking of his mother's cookies, his mouth watered. Four years of restaurants and fast food made him more than ready for home cooking. He wanted to be fussed over like Allison—

Andy wanted to stop his thoughts from going on that trip, but Allison's last request kept coming back. It was time for him to keep his promise. A dedicated career woman who didn't want children might be the one for him. He'd try to be as happy with her as he had been with Allison. Allison would expect him to make that kind of a commitment.

Katherine Reese slid smoothly into his thoughts. After forgetting about her for years, he now thought of her often. He chuckled. One thing for sure, she was no longer the kid who used to follow him around.

He'd be only a backyard away from her. He wondered if Katherine would be pleased to have him as a neighbor again. His sister wrote that she dated Franklin Perry, his classmate and rival in high school. Andy grimaced. He would never like or admire the guy, no matter how many years went by. Still, Franklin was handsome and rich. He had a lot to offer a woman.

Only it didn't have to be Katherine. She deserved better.

But then, who was he to make such a judgment? People changed with the years, and even Franklin could have changed for the better. Whether he liked Franklin or not, he intended to bank with him.

Since Andy wanted his company to be within the village limits, the plot of ground next to the library appealed to him. Permission to build had to come from the village board. He planned to have his office building face Main Street, with his factory in the back. When he walked Katherine back to the library after the birthday party, the whole idea came to him.

Before he returned to Oregon, he got the information he needed for his venture. Since the land had been vacant for many years, he felt there would be no problem purchasing it.

In Oregon, he found an architect and gave him his plans. Visualizing the buildings gave Andy a warm feeling of pride.

Some people in Pine View would be surprised. He didn't go to college after high school as had his classmates. He went to Oregon to be with his Uncle Frank

19

and had started working with computers immediately. With Allison's encouragement, he had gotten his degree by taking night classes.

Andy never worried about what people thought of him. However, he wanted his parents to be proud of his accomplishments. Katherine's approval was a given.

It seemed natural for him to think of her. After all, he would be her neighbor once again. He recalled her as a small, thin girl, often smiling. Brown eyes and a head full of soft curls. Since his sister Mary and she were best friends, Katherine was always around. Thinking back, having his own fan club made up of Katherine, Mary and their friends stroked his ego. At football games, their cheers rose in a crescendo of encouragement from the stands. Katherine was so animated when his team won, and almost in tears when they lost.

Would Katherine cheer him on as enthusiastically in his new venture? He hoped so.

Later, that night, he picked up the phone.

"Hi, Mom."

"What's wrong?" came her breathless voice.

"Nothing's wrong. I wanted to talk to you."

"At two o'clock in the morning?" she demanded.

"Gosh, Mom, I forgot the time difference. Sorry."

"Well, since I'm awake, go ahead and talk to me."

Andy heard his mother telling his dad to go back to sleep. "It's only Andy. No time sense at all."

"How would you like a boarder?" Andy asked. "I want to come home for good."

His mother's joyful cry had his father asking what was the matter.

"Andy's coming home! Isn't that wonderful?" She then said to Andy, "Your room is always there, son. When are you coming?"

"Not for a few weeks. I'll let you know."

"What about your business?"

"I'm bringing it to Pine View. I'll tell you all about it later. Too complicated to go into it right now. Sorry about the time, Mom, but I had to tell you." He laughed. "I love you and I'll let you get back to sleep. Bye."

Andy leaned back in the chair. Calling his mother made it feel like he had burned his last bridge. He whistled cheerfully as he picked up the letters on his desk.

Happiness bloomed in his heart for the first time in years.

He was going home.

With her armful of books, Mrs. Stratton entered the library. The years had treated her kindly and she looked younger than her age. From her, Andy inherited his blue eyes and blond hair. His father contributed his tall, muscular body and easy charm.

Katherine smiled.

"Good morning, dear. I'm back for another supply of books," Mrs. Stratton said. "I really should do more housework than reading, but I'm addicted to my romance novels. Always love a happy ending."

"So do I."

"As I said many times before, you should be married

and have your own family instead of spending all your time in this library."

"Maybe someday. Thank goodness, I love my job."

"I've got great news. Andy's coming home to stay. I'm so happy. I've told him his room is always ready for him."

Katherine's heart leaped in her chest. Was there a chance her childhood wedding dream would come true? He would be living next door once more. She had assumed he was going to stay in Oregon for the rest of his life.

"That's . . . that's good news," she stammered. "When's he coming? What will he do when he comes? Job opportunities aren't plentiful in upstate New York."

"His former boss sold him his business. He'll manufacture computer chips."

Katherine didn't understand. "Here? In Pine View?"

"I guess so. He said it was too complicated to explain at two o'clock in the morning."

"He forgot the time difference?"

"You know Andy. He wanted to tell me the news." Mrs. Stratton smiled. "I'm sure he has planned it all out."

Yes, Katherine thought. Andy would have made his decisions and had a workable plan in place. That much Mary had told her about Andy over the years. She remembered his musings about the businesses along Main Street. He had said there was only one vacant lot, the one next to the library and the last one in the village.

A tiny chill crawled up her spine. Surely Andy wasn't thinking—but that property was hers! She wanted it for the library addition, and everyone in the village knew it.

But Andy probably didn't know her plans.

Thank heavens, the lot couldn't be big enough for a factory. Or could it? Imagine—she really couldn't—a *factory* in beautiful Pine View. Factories were found only in big cities. Never here!

"Do give my regards and best wishes to Andy." Not for the world would she reveal to Andy's mother her doubts. She checked out the books chosen by Mrs. Stratton. "You do read a lot."

"I told you my house suffers." She gave a laugh. "Even though Mary has her own house and is happily pregnant, she picks up the slack. She spoils me."

"You're easy to spoil," Katherine said. "Good-bye until the next time."

After Andy's mother left, Katherine doodled on the pad on her desk. She wondered if Andy had treated his wife like a queen, or if he had been a husband who expected to be waited on. Would she ever find out?

Longing filled her. She wanted to have Andy love her and be there for her. To tell her she was his all as he kissed her breathless. That he couldn't live without her . . .

She sighed deeply. Such thinking served no purpose. She closed the library. Her empty house held no charm for her tonight.

After the sudden death of her father, she had gotten

23

her librarian job and lived with her mother. Two years ago, her mother had gone to stay with her sister in Arizona because of her health. Katherine had adjusted to living alone and refused to give in to feeling sorry for herself.

Still under the spell of her earlier thoughts, and calling herself all kinds of a fool, she went up into the spacious attic of her house. In the far corner was an old trunk. She lifted the lid. The top tray held what she wanted. Very carefully she pushed back the tissue paper to reveal her grandmother's wedding gown. She gathered it up and carried it down to her bedroom.

Laying it out on her bed, she marveled at its handsewn beauty. It was heavy white satin with lace inserts on the full skirt and long train. Lace edged the high neckline. The long sleeves had tiny pearl buttons at the cuff.

She unbuttoned the long row of pearl buttons at the back of the gown and laughed. How frustrating they would be to the clumsy and hurried fingers of the bridegroom when . . . Never mind. She wouldn't let her imagination go any further.

Would the gown fit her?

With bated breath, she slipped it on. She held together the gaping back. The gown cupped her breasts and molded her figure as though it had been made for her. She twisted back and forth before the mirror, twitching the long train with ease. Oh, it was so beautiful. She carefully hung it at the back of her closet, using a plastic cover to protect it from dust and dirt. Another time she would find the veil.

All this in preparation for the day she'd marry the man she loved in this perfect gown.

Andy.

Always, he was the man in her dreams.

Chapter Three

Andy sat at his desk in Portland with the preliminary blueprints of his proposed office building spread before him. He rubbed his eyes and rotated his shoulders. His architect was working on the final plans for the factory building. That utilitarian structure and its parking lot wouldn't be seen from Main Street. He felt Katherine would favor putting the factory in the back and out of sight. He wanted Katherine's approval in a big way.

A small patch of lawn, the same size as the one in front of the library, was sketched in front of the office building. Andy admired the sleek design. The Stratton Computer Company would soon be a reality.

As with the factory building, he was making the office building big to allow for growth. When he opened the operation, he'd be able to employ one hundred people. He hoped for loyal and dependable workers. Together, they would help each other to provide for a happy life—in the best possible world, right in the village of Pine View.

He wasn't into making money in order to accumulate a fortune. He only wanted a good, comfortable life. Maybe he was being too idealistic, but he hoped not.

After he returned to Pine View it wouldn't be all work, as it had been in Oregon. He'd go to movies, ball games, and other fun places. His promise to Allison kept returning. It was time to fulfill it.

Andy looked again at the design before he rolled up the blueprints. For a second, he had a feeling something wasn't quite right. Something Katherine had said or pointed out? He shrugged the thought away.

A warm, happy feeling washed over him. It was going to be good to be with the family and all his old friends. Only now he realized that life in Oregon had lacked the closeness he felt in Pine View. He and Allison had had a circle of friends their own age. Most of them worked in the computer field and were just starting out in life. Had he married and lived in Pine View, he would have had the support of family and friends when Allison died. Everyone would have gathered around him and helped him through the stages of grief and loss. But he had managed by himself. He didn't need anyone to help him, then or now.

Katherine was on time for the monthly village meeting. She searched her closet for the most flattering dress she owned. She wanted to look her best tonight.

She chose a blue summer dress that swirled about her knees.

She nodded to the officers of the Village Preservation Society. As usual, they were seated in the front row, and there was an empty chair for her.

"I think I'll sit further back," she said to her friends.

She turned to face the room. The meeting room for the village of Pine View was on the first floor of the civic building. It was a barren room with no attempt to make it cheerful and inviting. No draperies were on the windows; the floor was splintered wood with not even a carpet runner up the aisle. Uncomfortable, wooden folding chairs were arranged on either side of the middle aisle.

Katherine started to walk to a seat in the third row. She looked ahead, and her heart almost skipped a beat. Andy was sitting in an aisle seat in the fifth row. His family filled in the rest of the row of seats. She hadn't known he was back in town.

He smiled, waving his hand, and she smiled back at him.

What was he doing here? She ignored the sudden uneasy feeling that crawled up her spine. She sat down in the end seat, knowing she wouldn't be able to look at him during the meeting. She was glad she had worn the blue dress. With effort, she focused on Mayor Tyler. She had the feeling Andy stared at her back, trying to make her turn and look at him. With effort, she didn't.

The mayor called the May meeting of the village board to order. Katherine let the usual business being conducted wash over her like a wave. Why was Andy here? The question nagged her. She wished the meeting would hurry up and get to her request. Tonight's expected vote of acceptance was all she needed.

"Please come to order." Mayor Tyler's bang of the gavel ended all conversations. "We have two building requests to vote on."

Two? Katherine sat straighter. Surely no one wanted her lot. It must be for a porch or something like that. Why did Andy come to mind? Once again, she concentrated on Mayor Tyler.

"As you know, Katherine Reese has requested permission to build an addition to the library. If this was the only request for this particular property, I'm sure she would get what she wants. However," Mayor Tyler paused significantly. He waited to get everyone's attention. "However, Andy Stratton has also submitted a request to build an office building to house his new Stratton Computer Company on the same plot of land."

Loud talking and exclamations of surprise burst out.

"Andy? Andy Stratton has a company?"

"Yeah, he's been out west a long time."

"Boy, I wonder how many jobs will be made."

"A big boost to the village . . ."

Then, a few people turned to Katherine and directed their remarks to her.

"Oh, Katherine, I'm sorry. I did want to see that addition."

"Katherine . . . I don't know what to say to you."

"But jobs are important . . ."

Mayor Tyler banged for attention.

"The board looked over Andy's blueprints in a special meeting prior to this one. However, we want you to learn more about his plans. We already know what Katherine's plans are," he said. "Andy, come up here."

Before Andy uttered a word, Katherine knew she had lost. By and large, jobs were more important than books. Supporting a family came first. The brief glance Andy gave her as he walked past her row was filled with consternation. She quickly turned her head away.

"Actually, I'm asking for a permit to build two buildings," Andy said. "The office building would front Main Street. The factory and parking lot will be in back of it. One hundred people will be employed in the manufacturing of computer chips. Ladies and gentlemen, I intend to stay in Pine View."

"Why do you want to build on that lot? Why not out of the village?" a board member asked.

"I want my employees to be able to walk to my company if they want to do so. I think everyone is sick and tired of driving miles to go to work."

Katherine agreed with those around her on this. Andy had given thought, underlined with compassion, to the welfare of those who would work for him.

"But Katherine had her request in before you, Andy. I think we shouldn't forget this." The complaint came from the secretary of the preservation society.

"That's right," called another voice.

The sound of the gavel restored silence.

"Please let Andy continue," Mayor Tyler ordered.

"After Andy has his say, we'll consider your wishes about our other request."

Questions as to the start of the construction of the two buildings, who would be employed, exactly what kind of benefits and the type of retirement plan were answered by Andy in a clear fashion, leaving no doubt Andy had a well thought out plan for his business.

Katherine admired Andy for answering every question.

"What happened to the employees of the company you bought in Oregon? Are they coming here?"

"I gave them that option. However, they didn't want to uproot their families. I worked with them to find other jobs."

With each answer, Katherine's dream of an addition became more hopeless. What Andy would be giving to the village was an economic boost. In the past, the village depended on the glove industry to provide jobs. With cheaper ones being made in foreign countries, gloves were no longer made in Pine View. Most villagers worked in neighboring cities. Though Andy would be starting small, there was great potential in bringing the aggressively growing computer industry to Pine View. Other companion companies might come into the area as well.

"Thank you, Andy."

When Andy went back to his seat, Katherine saw he didn't look at her. Nor did he look very happy. Could it be his conscience was bothering him since he knew— or had he not known—about her plans? After all, he had been away for years and been dependent upon his family to give him village news. Perhaps neither his mother nor Mary had told him about the proposed addition. It certainly wasn't exciting news. Whether he had known or not was of no consequence now. He had submitted his building request, and it would be voted on tonight. She would be defeated. With a start, Katherine brought her attention back to Mayor Tyler.

"Katherine Reese also has requested a building permit for the same lot. As you know, the library could do with an addition. The good feature is that the cost could be funded by a federal grant." The mayor paused. "Let's hear what you think."

In the discussion that followed, the support Katherine got pleased her. However, there was more support for Andy.

Finally, it was time to vote.

"Do I have a motion that we vote by secret ballot? Of course, give us a little time to get some ballots duplicated."

Katherine stood up and called out in a clear voice, "Mayor Tyler, that won't be necessary. I withdraw my request for a building permit. You'll need to vote only on Andy's request."

Katherine quickly sat down. She heard the loud gasps of surprise.

"Thank you, Katherine," the mayor said. "We appreciate what this means to you."

It didn't take long for the yes vote to be taken. The meeting ended soon after.

Katherine wanted to leave as quickly as possible. She accepted the condolences of her friends with a positive statement. "Isn't Andy's business a wonderful fortune for the village?" she said. "Of course, he should build where he thinks is best for all of us."

Then Andy blocked her way out the door.

"Katherine, I didn't know. I truly didn't know," he said.

"I believe you." Katherine gave him a rueful smile. "But even if you did know, I imagine you still would have put in your request. Now, be truthful, you would have."

"I would have had to think long and hard about it because I wouldn't want to hurt you," Andy said. "I'm glad I didn't have to make such a decision. This time, ignorance was bliss."

"I wish you every success. I'm proud of you." She tried to walk past Andy. He remained in the way.

"I'm sorry about your addition," he said. "Your heart must have been set on it. What will you do? Put another floor on the building?"

"Andy! That's impossible. The library is a historic house and can't be changed in that way," she explained, his suggestion striking horror to her soul. "I'll make do, somehow. I always can work things out. We'll just be more crowded than I like."

"If you need any help moving bookcases, let me know." He moved aside and Katherine walked past him.

"Good night, Andy," she said. There was no warmth in her voice and no smile on her lips. She felt she couldn't stand being in Andy's presence a moment longer. That he was to have her lot was a blow. His offer to move bookcases was so inadequate. As though that simple physical act would take care of everything.

After entering her house, Katherine went out to the patio. She wanted the quiet of the night to enter her soul and soothe her heart. Her gaze went to the heavens; she breathed in the fragrant air.

Andy didn't understand her and her needs, which should be no surprise to her. He didn't know her as a person. He only knew her as the kid next door and his sister's best friend. They had never gone out together, never dated, never talked.

Likewise, she didn't know him, either. He was a stranger. To make things difficult, she felt she loved him as much today as she had when she was a child. It made no logical sense, but there it was.

Depression descended on her like a fog. She didn't want to be a librarian forever. She longed to be married and have darling children. Children of her own instead of the ones who came to the library. Her life would be incomplete, a failure, if this never happened.

She recalled yesterday's lunch with Mary.

"Mary, you're so fortunate—happily married and now, best of all, pregnant," she said.

"Don't I know it," Mary answered. "Though Burt and I would have given all our love to an adopted baby, I'm thrilled to actually have my own." She patted her rounded middle. "The time can't pass fast enough for me. I want to hold my precious baby."

"I can almost imagine what you're going through. I ache to conceive a baby, to carry it inside of me, and to give birth to the son or daughter of the man I love," Katherine said, her words throbbing with passion.

"It'll happen to you. I know it will," Mary said, grabbing and squeezing Katherine's hand. "Franklin—"

"No, not Franklin." Katherine's interruption was quick and emphatic. Then she gave a short laugh. "I shouldn't say that. At least, not yet. The future is still before me, and I don't know whom I'll marry."

"I understand. You'll know when it's right for you. You've always known what to do and when to do it."

"I don't know about that. Lately, I've been mixed up. I'd like to have children before I get too much older. More than one, definitely. I was so lonely being an only child. Your family was great to include me in your family gatherings. I hope I won't have to wait until I'm in my forties before the right man comes along and I have my baby."

Mary laughed. "You goose. Of course you'll be married long before that."

"What are you now, a psychic and can look into the future?"

"Just using my common sense," Mary said. "Gosh, I better get going to meet Burt for that doctor's appointment."

The phone rang as soon as Katherine came in from the patio. She picked it up reluctantly, not wanting to discuss what had happened at the meeting.

"Mary," she said, "I didn't think it would be you. I was sure Mrs. Weber would be calling to commiserate with me."

"I'm going to do just that," Mary answered. "I'm in a dilemma. I'm happy for Andy, but I'm upset for you."

"Don't be. You know we Taurus women are made of stern, practical stuff," she said. "However, it was a shock. The meeting had a different ending than what I expected."

"Believe me. Andy didn't know anything about the addition. Neither Mother nor I e-mailed him about it. When he was home for Mother's party, the topic never came up." Mary went on, "He came back unexpectedly this afternoon. He told us about his company, but didn't say a word about his request for the building permit. Guess he wanted to be sure he had it. He feels badly about what happened to you."

"I do too, but don't worry. I'll make other plans for the library. Heaven knows we've gotten along so far with things as they are. We'll keep going." Katherine paused. "I'm curious, though. When did Andy decide to build in Pine View?"

"He got the idea the morning he walked back with you from the post office."

How vivid that morning was to Katherine. She had been happy to walk with Andy and harbor a hope that he would come back home and into her life.

"He never said anything to me," Katherine said softly.

"That's Andy. He can be very deep when he wants to

36

be. Sometimes I think he hides his inner feelings too much," Mary said. "As soon as he got to Oregon, he made his plans. When he makes up his mind to do something, nothing is going to stop him. He faxed his building request. To make sure things worked out, he flew home to be at the meeting."

"Fortunately for Pine View, he'll build here and provide needed jobs." Katherine didn't let her disappointment creep into her voice. "We'll talk more tomorrow."

"Sorry for talking so long. You get some rest."

After the phone call, Katherine felt too wound up to go to sleep. The herbal tea she made promised to soothe and relax her. Sinking into an easy chair, she put her feet on the ottoman. Cradling the cup of tea in both hands, she breathed in the fragrant mist. Slowly, the tea and her deep breaths made her relax.

Tonight she had had a big shock. How quickly one's life and plans could be turned upside down—truly in the blink of an eye. She had been so sure of the outcome of the village meeting.

She hadn't expected Andy to come back to Pine View. Although it would be easy to start hoping her childhood dream would come true, she had to face facts and stop being foolish. Andy had shown no romantic interest in her either in high school or since he became a widower. Being her neighbor and having his business next door to the library didn't ensure Andy's feelings would change.

If this state of affairs continued indefinitely, a change had to be made in her life. Although her mother had been grateful she had chosen to work in Pine View after her father died, she had urged her to apply to a bigger library in a big city.

"Dear, I worry about you. There aren't any future prospects for you in Pine View."

"I love it here. It's home."

"But," her mother persisted, "I want to see you happily married."

"Franklin and I—"

"Katherine!" her mother interrupted. "Please be very sure before you commit yourself to Franklin Perry. I know he's a successful banker and is as steady as a rock. He'll make some woman a wonderful husband and father, but I don't think—"

"Mother, I know what I'm doing."

Thinking back, Katherine wasn't sure at all today.

She could get another library job. The information she downloaded two weeks ago about the Library of Congress in Washington, D.C. appealed to her. She had been to Washington four times and loved the city. Libraries in Boston, Tampa and Houston also were possible choices. She laughed as she realized how different each city was and so far away from Pine View.

It would be strange and heartbreaking to leave the village she was born in and had lived in all her life. Could she be brave enough to do it? Would she, a country person, survive in a metropolitan area, crowded with people instead of trees and blue skies and her beloved Adirondack Mountains?

She had believed her life was here in Pine View.

Well, it needn't be. She could work happily in Washington or Boston or anywhere in the world.

Andy wouldn't be there, but then, look at the years he lived in Oregon while she lived contentedly in Pine View without him. She could do it again. After all, she had lots of practice doing so! But tonight, plans for a future away from Andy depressed her. She really didn't want to move away. She would do so as a last resort. Katherine straightened her shoulders. Giving up wasn't in her. Tomorrow would be a better day.

Katherine dreaded going to work the morning after the meeting. She'd be busier with talkers rather than readers. While waiting to have their books checked out, they would want to discuss the meeting and ask her how she felt. Most would be genuinely sorry for her. Still, their pity she could do without.

Before she left the house for work, the doorbell rang shrilly once, and then again, as though the caller was impatient.

"I'm coming," she muttered as she opened the door.

"Andy," she said, her eyes widening in surprise.

"I couldn't sleep last night," he said. "I'm sorry about getting your lot. I didn't know you wanted it. I'd never do anything to hurt you."

Katherine, seeing his bloodshot eyes and untidy hair, believed him.

"Come in," she said. "We have time for a cup of coffee. You look like you need one."

Andy followed her into the kitchen. The sun took

39

that moment to shine through the window, making the room cheerful and bright.

"I hope you aren't going to hold it against me. I never discussed my plans with the family. I wanted to surprise them." He sank into a chair. Without looking in the cup, he took a big gulp of coffee. He almost spit it out.

"It's black!"

Katherine laughed. "How should I know what you drink? That's the way I like it."

"Well, I don't."

Katherine got him the sugar and cream he wanted.

"Look, I'll drive you to the library. I'll show you the blueprints of the office building. I know you'll like it," he said. "They're in the car."

"I'd like to see them very much."

Was she going to hate the building? She hoped not. But men weren't great at thinking aesthetically about things. She also remembered it was going to be next to her lovely Victorian house.

Katherine bent her head to look closely at the top sheet of the blueprints. It showed the design of the front of the building. She didn't go any further. She didn't even want to see what was before her on page one—the drawing of Andy's pride and joy. He had rolled it out and kept it from snapping back with two books.

"Didn't the architect do a great job? I told him what I wanted," Andy said with pride.

Katherine turned her back to him. She closed her

Chapter Four

After lunch the next day the Village Preservation Society met in the conference room of the library. The members wondered what was so important that this meeting had to be called in the middle of the week and not on the regular meeting date. They waited for their president to start.

Katherine rapped the gavel for attention. "We have a problem."

"Has Mr. Burgess put up the wrong sign in front of the hardware store?" Mrs. Stone grumbled.

"I only wish it was that simple," Katherine answered. "Our new business, Stratton Computer Company, submitted the blueprints for their office building to the village board. Andy showed them to me yesterday."

"I think it's a shame that you can't have your addition to the library," Mrs. Stone said. "You had plans submitted long before Andy decided to build there."

"But we need the new company," Nellie Gray said in a loud voice. "More than a hundred people will be working there."

"That's right. Jobs are more important than books."

Katherine rapped the gavel hard on the pad.

"Ladies, please, let's get back to business," Katherine said, a tremor in her voice. It hurt to be told she wasn't important. Well, at least her job wasn't. She did understand the work situation in the village. Hadn't she gotten behind Andy's proposal at the meeting?

"The board gave Andy permission to build, and I've accepted their decision. What I'm objecting to—well, what we all should consider—is the façade of the proposed business building."

Katherine held up a sketch of it she had made.

"You can see it's a very modern building, made mostly of concrete, plate glass, and chrome!"

General murmuring and talking broke out.

"It's so big . . . it sure is a modern building . . . it's so square . . ."

"Ladies, this building doesn't meet our specifications. It is being built on Main Street and needs to conform with the other businesses. It has to look *Victorian*, not modern." Katherine paused to let her statement sink in. "What are we going to do?" she prodded.

"I make a motion our president go to Andy and speak to him. Make him change the design of the front of the building." Nellie Gray sank back into her seat.

"I second the motion," Mrs. Stone spoke up quickly.

Katherine had no choice but to ask for the vote. A unanimous "aye" was no surprise. Why had she ever been foolish enough to become president for a third term? Now she had to deal with Andy by herself.

"I, as president, will do as you order," Katherine said. She didn't smile at her friends. She felt they had deserted her and ordered her to do what they wanted no part of. They would let her confront a determined male.

"If there is no further business, we are adjourned."

Katherine said good-bye and waited until all had left. She dreaded carrying out the assignment. Andy was bound to be irritated. She wasn't sure he would take seriously any suggestions from a group of women who had no legal clout. All the businesses and merchants on Main Street in Pine View had been persuaded, one way or another, to have the Victorian theme carried out. Ultimately, they didn't resist the pressure placed on them because it was good for business.

With Andy, he wasn't selling anything or serving the public. He had no incentive to bow to the society's dictates. What did changing blueprints entail? Was it expensive? Though construction hadn't started, she didn't know if materials had been ordered.

Katherine felt a headache coming. She took a deep breath. She'd go right away to see Andy. It was only 3:30 and he would be in the temporary office he had over Denby's Drug Store, across the street from the library.

She had been very conscious he was so near to her—

45

both at work and at home. While walking to and from the post office, she didn't look up at the front window of his office for fear of drawing his attention. But she couldn't stop her heart from beating faster when she met him on the sidewalk or in the grocery store. He often crossed the street to walk with her, to her secret delight. He had also made it a habit to come into the library at least once a day.

Yesterday, he said, "I'm returning one of Mother's books." No smile curved his lips but a twinkle was in his eyes.

Then he leaned over the desk toward her. His head was so close his lips could brush her cheek if she dared to move closer to him. She didn't dare, and the opportunity was lost.

Leaving her assistant in charge of the library, Katherine walked up the narrow stairs to the second floor of Denby's Drug Store. Her steps sounded loud on the worn wood. No one could sneak up and surprise Andy. By now, he knew he was about to have a visitor. Katherine knocked on the door with its peeling paint and hand-lettered cardboard sign saying STRATTON COMPUTER COMPANY.

Andy opened the door.

"Ah, Katherine, do come in," he said with a big smile. "I saw you cross the street and was hoping you were coming to see me instead of going to the drug store."

Katherine felt her cheeks getting warm. His charm touched her like the kiss of a light breeze.

"Thanks. It's always nice to be welcome."

"You? Always." Andy's caressing voice was a double assault on her response to him. She took in a deep breath.

Katherine quickly sat down in the straight chair in front of the desk. Andy seated himself behind it. He pushed some papers into a haphazard pile that threatened to fall to the floor. Katherine resisted reaching over and establishing order.

"So, Katherine, what business do we have to discuss? Surely Mother doesn't have an overdue book that must be returned immediately."

Katherine saw the effort he made to look serious. "You've looked at all the buildings on Main Street," she said.

"Well, yes. So?"

"They all look alike in a certain way." Katherine found it hard to get to the point.

"Yeah, they all look nice," Andy agreed. "Just what are you trying to tell me?"

"I, that is, the Village Preservation Society, want you to change the design of the front of your office building."

Andy's eyebrows rose.

"What? Change the design? Why? I thought you liked it."

"As a modern building, the design is perfect, but your building has to look like all the Main Street businesses. They have a Victorian façade. Your modern one is out of place."

"Okay. I'll add some flower boxes like theirs," he said, a grin curving his lips.

"No, that isn't enough. You'd still have all that plate glass, chrome, and concrete."

"No."

"What do you mean by 'no?'" Katherine's voice rose an octave. "We haven't even discussed the issue."

"Most of the material has been ordered and paid for," he said. "The plans can't be changed without me losing a lot of money."

"I don't believe—"

"Believe it, Katherine." Andy leaned forward. All of his light-hearted grins were replaced by a tight-lipped seriousness. "I'm not being difficult, but business is business. I can't throw money away at this time. I won't be able to generate income until after the factory is built. Because I'm paying top dollar and bonuses, we start construction June 1 and hope to be finished by September."

Katherine's heart fell. Andy was right on this one point. Money was always a big issue. But when she thought of the glass and concrete, she cringed. A few flowers weren't going to make much difference.

"The flower boxes won't do it," she insisted. "You have to get the architect do something different that wouldn't cost much."

"Sorry, but I can't change the plans." Andy's tone was decisive.

Katherine stood up and walked to the door, her head held high. When Andy acted so stubborn and impossible, she wondered why she continued to love him. She should have her head examined.

Andy was there to open the door for her.

"Still friends?" His most beguiling smile washed over her.

Katherine didn't smile back. "Good-bye, Andy. This isn't over by a long shot."

She quickly left him. She wondered if the ladies would have to parade on the street with protest signs. She shuddered for putting out into the universe such a revolutionary thought in staid Pine View. It was the last thing she wanted to see happen.

At the window Andy watched Katherine's return to the library. He saw, as though for the first time, that it was a Victorian house. His modern office building would look out of place beside it.

He kicked the leg of a chair. He wanted to please Katherine, today and always. She was in his thoughts constantly.

Although he sure didn't have any ideas on how to change the front of his building, he'd talk it over with his architect. He'd even get in touch with his friend who worked on movie sets. Maybe he could suggest a cheap, false front!

A week later Andy walked into the library.

The sun shined through the diamond-paned windows to make patterns on the polished floor. The bookcases were like soldiers standing at attention. The fragrance from the vases of flowers Katherine scattered around the rooms combined with the musty scent of books.

Katherine swiveled her chair to face the front and to greet Andy. A flush of pleasure filled her. Happiness like an electric current hummed through her veins. She hadn't talked to him since their confrontation about his design. She had missed him more than she would ever confess.

"Good morning, Andrew," she said. She saw the twinkle in his eyes and the smile he quickly hid at her formal salutation. Her attempt to show she was provoked with him didn't work.

"Good morning, Sunshine," he said with a laugh.

Katherine laughed with him. It was no use being serious with Andy. She remembered he had always clowned around and made people laugh.

"What can I do for you? No books to be returned?" she asked.

"Not today. I heard from my architect and an old friend. They came up with several ideas to make you and your society happy. That is, if you approve," he said.

He leaned on the desk, bringing his head close to hers. For a breathless moment, Katherine thought how easy it would be for her to kiss him. She leaned closer to him. Then she realized what she was doing and pulled back. Whatever was she thinking? No way did she want Andy to think she was chasing after him. Every available woman in town was in line.

"So, tell me." She rolled her chair to the left, away

from his tempting lips. She moved some books on her desk.

"Since we've already started digging the foundation, the building will have to be where we planned. We're ahead of schedule. The only space we can work with is the area I thought would match the lawn in front of the library."

Andy reached over for a pad of paper on the desk. He made a rough sketch of the proposed building and a block to represent the library.

"It's a good thing Mother had a snapshot of the library," Andy said. "It helped the architect. He put a porch in front with all that fancy decoration on top— think you call it gingerbread trim—and a banister in keeping with the one you have on your porch. The double front doors will be oak with beveled glass inserts."

"That's wonderful. So much better than only the flower boxes you suggested." Katherine smiled at Andy.

"Wait. There's more. Wood shingles to cover the concrete as well as shutters on the upstairs windows. And," with a bow, Andy said, "my suggestion."

He quickly sketched in a widow's walk on the top of his building. "Mike Spencer's house has one of these, and I thought it was great."

With a joyful cry, Katherine ran around the desk and threw her arms around Andy, hugging and kissing him again and again.

"How absolutely perfect. I never imagined you'd be able to do this. Thank you, thank you so much," she said and kissed him again.

Andy held her tightly and returned each kiss with increasing heat. When she tried to break away, he kept her in his arms.

"If it only takes making a few changes in a blueprint to make you kiss me, I've got to come up with another plan," he teased.

Katherine shifted in his arms. "Get serious, Andy."

"Never. I like to be thanked this way." He pulled her closer to him, and a chuckle rumbled out. "Give me another one for good measure."

This time his kiss was hard and demanding but warm, making her long for more than just kisses. This kiss lifted their relationship to another level. She felt Andy responding to it.

"Excuse me," uttered a voice behind them.

With a start, the two parted.

"Andy brought me good news," Katherine explained, her voice a mere whisper.

Andy laughed. "I'm always a bearer of good news," he said in his defense to the smiling woman at the front of the desk.

Katherine retreated behind the desk and sat down. "Be sure to tell your architect and friend how pleased you've made me."

Andy gave her a wink and a grin. "Sure thing. I won't keep you from your work," he said. He turned to the woman handing in her books. "Good day, and nice meeting you. We'll meet again, I'm sure."

He smiled at her, and she returned his smile. It always fascinated Katherine to see Andy's charm at work.

Andy waved to both of them and left.

Katherine sighed happily. What a wonderful day this had turned out to be. Andy had done the impossible. She believed he made the changes to please her and make her happy—not because the preservation society had some rules. She hugged the knowledge to her heart.

"Let me help you find your book," she said to Mrs. Hughes.

Chapter Five

Although she would have been happier to have Andy call her, Katherine accepted Franklin's invitation to dinner on Saturday night at Stone Inn. For years she and Franklin had accompanied each other to different functions at their convenience. Neither thought of it as a "date." Tonight was no exception.

She was startled by Franklin's unexpected compliment.

"You're lovely tonight," Franklin said, his gaze roaming over her.

Katherine's cheeks flushed pink. Her mother's pearls and drop earrings went well with the pale yellow chiffon dress with its scooped neckline. She had swept her hair back from her cheeks and caught it in a flowered ring to fall in soft waves down her back.

Franklin's words bolstered her self-esteem that had

been low for the last two weeks. Andy was so busy with the construction of his office building that he didn't drop in to visit her. A cheerful wave was all she got. His mother returned her own books.

Unfortunately, it was easy to imagine Andy with Melissa, his old girlfriend. Since Melissa was twice divorced and Andy was a widower, they were both free to start again. Just because she dreamed about him after putting a piece of cake under her pillow so many years ago didn't mean she was any closer today to marrying Andy as she was before.

Tonight, because of her mood and his attention, she thought of Franklin's good points. They did get along well together. Franklin was well read and their discussions on various books were lively. He remembered the holidays and celebrated them with her. However, that was as far as it went with her. She didn't love him.

She admitted that love, after all, had many varied forms. In fact, there were a multitude of versions of love that could grow and wake up in people's lives. It was time for her to think about this, to stop fantasizing in a childish manner as she had been doing. She had believed for years that Andy would marry her because, for heaven's sake, she dreamed he would. As though a piece of wedding cake—ordinary cake—had mystical, psychic powers to predict the future. It really was ludicrous and foolish.

Tonight did prove she didn't want Franklin to change the status quo and knew she had made an unwise move on her part.

They were halfway through their dinner before the waiter seated the diners at the next table. Katherine stared and Franklin definitely uttered an oath under his breath.

Andy and Melissa.

They made a striking couple. Melissa's long black hair and flamboyant red, strapless dress was a perfect foil for Andy's blond good looks.

"Why, hello there," Melissa said. "Isn't this a pleasant surprise?"

"Hi, Melissa and Andy," Katherine answered with a forced smile. To see Andy with Melissa was an unpleasant shock. "Yes, it is a surprise."

"We can recommend the steak tonight," Franklin said without a smile.

"I'll consider having it," Andy said. He didn't smile at Franklin either. He turned to pull out Melissa's chair. "We won't keep you from your dinner."

Then each couple ignored the other by giving undivided attention to their dinner.

It was, however, a relief to Katherine when Franklin rejected having a dessert.

"None for me, either," she told the waiter.

After bidding Andy and Melissa good night, they left.

Katherine saw that Franklin had managed to hold in his feelings while at the inn. Once they reached the car his tirade broke out.

"That sister of mine! She knows how I feel about Andy, and still she goes out with him. And she knew we

56

were coming to the inn. She made Andy bring her here tonight."

"Franklin!" Katherine exclaimed. "I'm sure that isn't the case at all. The inn is the best restaurant around here and Andy—"

"Andy! He's another one who likes to make my life miserable."

Katherine laughed. Franklin was being absurd.

"Come on, Franklin. Forget your annoyance with Melissa and Andy. They didn't deliberately conspire to ruin your evening."

Katherine talked easily of this and that on the way home.

"Come into the kitchen," she said, "and I'll make some coffee. This morning I made a chocolate cake which I remember you like," she said. "Make yourself at home."

Franklin took off his jacket and draped it on the back of the chair. A few minutes later he said, "This cake is delicious. I'm glad you gave me a big piece."

Katherine smiled at him. A short time later they settled on the couch for their customary book discussion.

"What's your opinion of the latest best seller?" she asked. She knew the rest of the evening would be spent exchanging views and even having some disagreements. She, for one, wouldn't think of what Andy and Melissa might be doing.

After Andy pulled into his parents' driveway, he sat in the car thinking about the evening.

When he came into the inn with Melissa, he saw Katherine smiling at Franklin across the table. Dismay filled him. He didn't want Katherine to be with Franklin and he didn't want her acting as though she liked being with him. Then sanity kicked in as he realized that he was there with Melissa. Katherine had every right to go out with anyone she chose.

What had Katherine thought? She seemed polite enough, but the warmth left her face when she spoke to Melissa.

Though he hoped he hadn't made a fool of himself, he couldn't keep his eyes or thoughts off Katherine and Franklin being together. It had been a relief to see them leave. On one level, he tried to entertain Melissa. On another level, he was conscious of every look and smile Katherine directed at Franklin. He had no reason to resent Franklin who had every right to be with Katherine. He didn't understand what was going on inside of himself, but he knew he resented Katherine being with Franklin—or any other guy.

To cover up his new and disturbing feelings for Katherine, he urged Melissa to go dancing after dinner. Then he found he wanted to dance with Katherine and hold her in his arms—not Melissa! It was crazy. Why had he taken Melissa dancing? He had given Melissa all the wrong signals and been dishonest. Sure, they had a good evening together, but only as friends. The predatory gleam in Melissa's sultry glances made him uncomfortable. While dancing, her body clung to him.

It shocked him to realize that he wanted to have Katherine cling to him.

By the time he took Melissa home, she had sensed his coolness for her. He deserved her cold good-bye.

He remembered his promise to Allison to remarry. How easily he thought of Katherine. When had she grown up and become a beautiful woman? It was only yesterday he called her Half-pint and thought of her only as his sister's best friend. A "little" friend, at that.

Half-pint.

Katherine had gasped the time he used it before. What was it about that nickname that nagged at him? What was so special about it? He frowned. No use forcing the memory. He'd eventually remember it.

Andy got out of the car. He was tempted to walk to the back of the house and look toward Katherine's house. Would he be able to see Katherine and Franklin on the patio?

He shook his head. A very bad idea.

Instead, he walked into the dark house and to his room. He and Melissa would only be friends. This much had been made clear to him tonight.

Katherine hurried into the library on Monday morning. She stopped short in surprise.

"Where did you come from?"

A fluffy black cat, resembling a big dust mop, lay on the blotter on her library desk. She looked up at Katherine, purring with all her might. She acted very much at home. When Katherine scratched her under her white chin, she purred louder. She kneaded the scratch pad on the desk with her white-tipped paws.

"Hey, who's your friend?"

Katherine jumped and jerked her head around to see Andy standing a few feet away. She hadn't heard him enter the library.

"Haven't a clue. I don't even know how she got in here."

"She?"

"Well, I don't know the sex. I just assumed so because she's a beautiful Persian cat and doesn't have scars or bitten ears like a tomcat would."

"Easy to find out." Andy picked up the cat. "It's a she," he said. He stroked the cat in his arms. She was content to stay there.

"Sure is a friendly animal. What are you going to do with her?"

"First, I want to find out how she got in here. I thought I locked up yesterday."

Katherine walked to the back of the big room. Looking over her shoulder, she saw Andy still holding the cat. He bent down and rubbed his cheek on her head. The sight pleased Katherine. A different side to this macho male, she thought. Weren't men mostly partial to dogs? Not Andy, evidently. She liked learning something new about him.

"Ah, here it is," she called back to Andy.

He came, still holding the cat.

"I left this patio window open."

The Wedding Cake

At that moment, the cat jumped out of Andy's arms, leaped to the windowsill, and left the library.

"Well," Katherine exclaimed. "I wonder why she even came in if she was in such a hurry to leave again."

"You know what they say about cats," Andy said. "They're mysterious creatures. If you keep the window open, maybe she'll come back."

"Leave a window open? Not on your life. Anyone could come in." Katherine slammed the window shut and locked it. "Besides, such a beautiful cat must belong to someone. She's not a starved stray."

"Do you have a cat?"

"Not at the moment. Oscar died of old age last month. I miss him very much, but I'll wait before I get another one."

Katherine walked away from Andy. She didn't want him to see the tears she blinked away. She had had Oscar for fourteen years. His death had been hard to take. Andy must have forgotten about him. But then, there was little Andy remembered about their early years. She had to stop expecting him to recall events that were still so real to her.

"What can I do for you, Andy? Haven't seen much of you lately."

Andy's hands were in his jean pockets. His T-shirt was stained and had several holes in it. He had been to work early today. He was looking at a row of books in one of the bookcases. Since the books were on cooking and home economics, Katherine didn't think they were for his personal reading. She hid her smile.

Andy came to the front desk and faced Katherine. She gazed up at him, her hands no longer busy stacking the books that had been scattered on the desk. Her mouth became dry, and her heart gave an erratic thump. There was no one else in the library at this early hour. The very air seemed to vibrate between them.

Andy finally spoke.

"Are you busy on Wednesday night? I'd like to take you to the movies," he said.

Chapter Six

Katherine gave a little gasp. Andy was asking her out on a date! Her spirit soared with joy. This could be the beginning of the relationship she had been longing for.

"Movie? Wednesday?"

"A small movie theater in Bradford features classic movies. This week it's *The Scarlet Pimpernel*." Andy grinned. "I thought you'd like to see it."

"It must be in black and white. My, I'd forgotten all about that one," Katherine said. "Leslie Howard plays the lead. Of course, he's best known for his role as Scarlett's love in *Gone with the Wind*."

"Yeah, well, will you go with me?" Andy didn't remember any of these facts and felt uncomfortable. He realized how far apart in interests he and Katherine were. After he left Pine View, they had seen little of each other. Katherine was immersed in the world of books; his interests were in computers and sports. What would they talk about on a date? He hadn't given that a thought. He truly didn't know anything about Katherine—except that he was drawn to her and wanted to be near her all the time. He liked just looking at her beautiful face and relaxing in her serenity.

He waited for her answer, holding his breath. He felt like a teenager again, agonizing that the answer would be "no."

"Yes, I'd like to go," Katherine said. "What time will you pick me up?"

Andy's breathing returned to normal.

"Great. I'll be there at six-thirty," Andy said. "I'm glad you're coming with me. I'll be seeing you."

He seemed about to say something else but didn't. He headed for the front door. Katherine wondered if he was afraid to stay longer in fear she would change her mind. A foolish thought. Andy afraid of anything—especially of his charm with women? It couldn't be.

Katherine leaned back in her chair.

A movie date, after all these years, with Andy Stratton.

Had it really happened? How often she had dreamed of such a date. If it had occurred years ago, the movie would be shown at the small Pine View Theater on Bridge Street. They would have bought popcorn and sat in the small balcony like all the other couples.

Unfortunately, the theater had burned to the ground. Now villagers had to go out of town or rent a movie and watch it at home. Bradford was twenty miles away. She wondered why Andy chose that particular theater. Would he even be interested in an old romantic movie? She hoped he would like the show. She would have thought he would choose an action and adventure film. Even if it seemed out of character for him, she was happy with his movie selection.

Andy hurried across the street and took the stairs two at a time to his temporary office. He couldn't believe his good luck. He had to be sure to thank Mary. He suggested taking Katherine to the latest adventure movie, but Mary squashed that idea.

"Katherine would hate it. Take her to a romantic one," Mary said.

"Where would I find one?"

Good thing Mary had all the answers. He looked at his computer. Just the source for him to learn about Leslie Howard and the movie. The story about the French Revolution was interesting, but personally, he liked the lead character to have some visible muscles. But it would be hard to expose them in those fancy costumes. He also read about *Gone with the Wind*. He admired Rhett Butler much more than the weak Ashley. For a strong, independent woman, Scarlett didn't know squat about men. Thinking of Franklin, he hoped Katherine had better judgment than Scarlett.

Andy looked out the window to watch the construction of his office building. Katherine and the library patrons had to contend with the noise. He hadn't considered the noise factor at all and felt guilty about it.

Katherine hadn't complained. His admiration of her increased daily. And he very much liked looking at her. All curvy and soft in the right places. She was a very desirable woman.

After turning off his computer, Andy crossed the street to check on the construction. At least when the factory building went up, the noise wouldn't affect the library as much. September 1 couldn't come fast enough. He had orders for his computer chips as soon as he was operational.

He felt good about himself and the progress in his life. His move back to his hometown was the best one he could have made. In both his business and his growing relationship with Katherine things were going well. His guilt-ridden nightmares about Allison's death came rarely these days.

Her movie date with Andy made Katherine feel as giddy as a teenager. She wanted to dance around the room, hugging herself in delight. At least, that was what she would have done during her school years. Being a sedate twenty-eight year old woman, she did it in spirit only.

"You look so happy," Mrs. Stone observed.

"It's such a beautiful day," she answered. "However, I'm looking forward to the day next week when this horrible noise will stop."

"Yes," Mrs. Stone shouted over the sudden burst of a jack hammer. "It's terrible. I'm getting out of here." She waved good-bye and left.

Before Katherine locked up that night she found a copy of *The Scarlet Pimpernel*. When she read it long ago, she had sighed over the romance and looked forward to having a dashing hero in her life. One who would risk his life for her. It was easy to imagine blond Andy in the role of such a hero.

At the last minute, she checked the window near the patio to make sure it was closed. She wondered to whom the beautiful black cat belonged. She had never seen it near the library. She would have liked to adopt her now that Oscar was gone. Katherine smiled thinking of how Andy had cradled the cat in his arms and stroked her until she purred with pleasure. A big, virile man like Andy. A man who could make her content to be in his arms too.

The cat sat on her desk once more the next morning.

"Well, how did you get in this morning? I know I locked up last night."

The cat gazed at Katherine with her green eyes wide open. Then she ignored her in order to lick her paw and slowly wash her face.

"I haven't any cat food for you, so I hope someone has already given you breakfast," Katherine said. Then she laughed at herself. Carrying on a conversation with a cat as though she could understand every word she uttered.

"So you decided to get a cat," Andy said.

"How do you do that?" Katherine turned to face him. "What?"

"Sneak up on me so quietly."

Andy shrugged his shoulders. "I'm a quiet kind of guy."

"Sure you are." It was a pleasurable shock to have him so close that she felt his heat and smelled his after-shave.

Should she tack a little bell on the door to warn her of the entrance of a patron? No, she decided, it would annoy her by the end of the day.

"I have no idea how the cat got in this time," she said. "Want to help me look for it?"

A windowpane in the corner of the cellar had fallen out. Fortunately, it hadn't broken.

"I'll get some tape and you can help me fix it," she said.

"Of course. I'm the handyman for you. Call on me anytime." He grinned at her. "And I mean anytime, day or night."

Katherine smiled at him. Oh, how she wanted to call him—to have him come to her in the moonlight and take her in his arms. To have him love her—anytime, day or night.

She turned away from him. It was hard to get back to real life.

The window fixed, they left the basement.

The cat was now curled into a ball and asleep on the desk. A shaft of sunshine fell on her, and she looked as though she would be there for the duration of her nap.

"How am I supposed to get my books checked in?" Katherine complained.

"Pick her up and put her somewhere else," Andy said.

"But I hate to disturb her."

"You're too soft-hearted. Let me."

Andy picked up the cat and laid her on the couch before the fireplace. The cat yawned and settled down without a protest.

"Thanks," she said. "I'll do that the next time."

"Call on me to rescue you from invading cats," Andy said. He sat on the edge of the desk, acting in no hurry to leave.

She reached for the books Mrs. Stone was handing to her. There was a burst of noise next door.

"Andy assures me that the noise will end next week," Katherine said to Mrs. Stone.

"Well, Andy, you better keep your word," Mrs. Stone said as she walked toward the fireplace to pet the cat. "Queenie looks right at home here. Mr. and Mrs. Bennett were wondering where she disappeared to since old Mrs. Bennett had to go to the nursing home."

"She came in yesterday and today for a short time. If they're looking for a home for her, I'll be glad to take her," Katherine said.

Andy leaned over to Katherine. "Didn't I tell you you're soft-hearted," he said in her ear, his breath fanning her cheek. Katherine felt a warm flush pink her cheeks. Andy's remark was a compliment, not a criticism. She smiled at him, not knowing his heartbeat quickened.

"May I have my book?" Mrs. Stone asked, looking

from one to the other. "When I go there for lunch today, I'll ask the Bennetts. I don't think they'll object to you taking Queenie. They have four cats of their own as it is."

At the door Mrs. Stone said, "Queenie is very spoiled, especially about what she'll eat. You may not think this is such a good idea at all."

Katherine laughed. "I know all about how finicky a cat can be. Oscar was a prime example. I'll bring over some cans of food at noon and try them out. Call me after lunch and let me know if I'm a cat owner again."

"You'll hear from me," Mrs. Stone said and left.

There was a sudden loud burst of construction noise. Over the din, Andy's laughter was lost.

When there was a lull in the noise, Andy said, "I hate to leave." To her surprise, he leaned over the desk and kissed her cheek. "Duty calls, but I'll be back again. Bye." He winked at her and strolled from the building.

For the rest of the afternoon, Katherine relived Andy's gentle kiss on her cheek and his words. Did he really want to be with her? How serious was the kiss? Her imagination threatened to run away with her. The ringing of the phone ended her flight into fancy.

"I can have the cat? Thank you, Mrs. Bennett. Do tell your mother that she'll have a good home with me. When I come to visit her, I'll bring Queenie too."

She gathered Queenie into her arms and hugged her. The cat's green eyes gazed into hers.

"Can I pet her?" a small voice behind her asked.

Katherine saw her after-school group had come in.

70

"Of course, you each may. This is Queenie and I'll bring her every day. She adopted me."

"How did that happen?"

Katherine answered the questions about the coming of the cat into her life. Fortunately, there was little noise from the construction site next door. Last week she had had to shout to be heard. The children, however, took it in stride, and even enjoyed the way she had to speak loudly. When the noise stopped without warning and she found herself still shouting, the children laughed hilariously.

Andy had come into the library and leaned against a bookcase, listening to her story hour. He laughed with the children. Like always, Andy appeared without warning. She hoped he came because he just had to see her.

After she opened the door on Wednesday night, Katherine smiled up at Andy. His gaze swept over her, and she laughed at his low whistle. She had on a yellow sundress with a square neck and small puffed sleeves. It fit her perfectly. She basked in the admiration in Andy's eyes.

"You're going to make it hard for me to look at the screen," Andy said.

"You'll like the movie," Katherine said hurriedly. She longed to believe Andy's compliment, but had to remember Andy's charm with women was a given.

In the car she quickly launched into "do-you-remember" situations that made them laugh all the way to Bradford.

The movie theater was almost empty.

"Sorry," Andy said, "I must have made a wrong choice."

"No, you didn't," Katherine said. "I wanted to see this movie again. I'm sure I'll enjoy it even more than I did in eighth grade."

They took seats in the middle. Andy bought sodas and a big carton of buttered popcorn. When he settled his arm around her shoulders, contentment filled Katherine.

Here in the dark theater, it was okay to feel and dream. This was a real date with the man she adored. Her own scenario began to unwind . . . He would touch her because he couldn't resist her. Soon, when she turned her face toward him, he would kiss her—a long, lingering kiss filled with passion . . .

When Andy whispered in her ear, Katherine was so swept up with her own story, she gasped.

"That Leslie guy is doing a good job of acting like a sissy. No one would suspect he's the real hero." He laughed. "It's a good thing I got on the Internet and found out what this movie is about. I guess I skipped it at school."

Katherine never went back to her romantic scenario. She answered Andy's questions about certain scenes. When their hands met in the popcorn carton, he looked at her and smiled. His arm around her shoulder tightened, and he drew her closer to him.

She gave a little sigh of contentment. This part was exactly as she had dreamed it would happen to her someday. If only it meant as much to Andy. If only he'd whisper the words she wanted to hear. But he didn't. Still, it was a night to remember with joy.

"How about a big sundae?" he asked when they left the theater. "Nedrick's always had great ones if I remember correctly."

"Sounds heavenly."

At her door, Andy said, "Tonight was great. We'll have to do it again."

She handed him the key. Suddenly, she was locked in his strong arms. She threw her arms around his neck and her fingers played with his soft hair. She looked into his eyes for a long moment before she lowered her lashes. Her lips raised in invitation. His warm lips brushed hers, then pulled away only to come down again with all the passion she had once dreamed of. Though she wanted this moment to last forever, Katherine stepped back.

"Good . . . good night, Andy," she said, her voice low and breathless as her heart continued to flutter. "Thanks for a lovely night at the movies."

Andy smiled down at her. "This is only the beginning for you and me. Count on it."

His gaze held her for a moment before he kissed her again. The kiss was light and tender. Afterward, he brushed her cheek with his knuckles.

"We'll definitely do this again," he said. Before he closed the door, he called softly, "Pleasant dreams."

Inside, Katherine leaned back against the door. Her hand touched her lips. The thrill of his kisses remained. Dare she count on his promise that this was only the beginning?

He wished her pleasant dreams. Was he hoping they would be of him? If at all possible, they would be.

She took a deep breath and sighed with contentment. This had been the best night of her life.

Chapter Seven

"How's the mother-to-be?" Andy asked his sister. "I know you'd love chocolate-covered cherries, but I brought you a basket of fruit instead."

Mary returned Andy's hug.

"Thanks. I can't believe I'm getting so big. Before long, you won't be able to hug me."

"How much longer?" he asked. Mary's pregnancy brought back the past, and he was afraid for her. It had come as a shock because Mary and her husband Burt had given up on having children. They had been pursuing adopting.

"Only four more months," Mary said. "The time is flying by, actually. I'm still sewing some clothes rather than buying them. This is a very special baby."

"You're going to be a great mom," Andy said.

He had thought the same thing of Allison. He

pushed the thought away. The death of his wife and son still haunted him. And fear for his sister was increasing no matter how hard he tried to repress it. He believed he was guilty of Allison's death. This guilt festered inside him. He had almost buried it in the dark recesses of his mind, but Mary's pregnancy brought it back to him.

What happened to Allison could happen to Mary. Andy didn't question his sister about her health, not wanting to hear any bad news. To all appearances, all was well. God, he hoped so.

"Come and see what I've done in the nursery. Burt thinks I'm going crazy, but I don't care."

Decals of cowboys on horses pranced on the walls.

"You must be expecting a boy," Andy said with a grin.

"I couldn't wait. I had to find out what we're having. Burt is as pleased as he can be." She turned to her brother and asked, "Did you—"

Andy quickly answered, "No, we didn't want to know."

Mary hurried to the kitchen counter. "Gosh, I'm sorry. That was thoughtless. I didn't mean to bring back sad memories."

"That's okay. Hey, are you going to give me a cup of coffee? I've got to get to my building." Andy sat down at the counter.

"How's the construction coming? Mother said the noise is terrible in the library."

Andy nodded his head. "I know. She wants me to

stop it. She thinks the workers could be quieter if they tried harder."

"You're almost finished with the exterior?"

"Yes, and that will take care of most of the problem. I'm glad the work has gone well and faster than planned." Andy stirred his coffee. "I've checked in the library, and Katherine has been very good about it."

Mary grinned. "Yes, I've heard about your visits."

Andy threw up a hand. "Don't you start. Mother's bad enough."

"I like Katherine," Mary protested.

"I do too." He laughed. "Yeah, we also had a good time together at the movies. She's easy to be with."

"Katherine's throwing a baby shower for me on Saturday night."

"That's nice."

"You should drop in later and see all the gifts."

"I'll see."

"What about Melissa?" Mary persisted in learning about her brother's personal life.

"She's a friend and that's it," Andy said. "Lay off, Sis, you know I'm too busy to bother with women."

Mary laughed. "Oh, sure."

She suddenly clutched her stomach and groaned.

"What's the matter?" Andy rushed to her side. "What's happening?"

Mary patted her stomach in a circular motion. "The baby gave me a big kick that time. Want to feel?"

"No." He backed away. "Are you sure it's only that? I can take you to Dr. Preston right away."

"I'll be okay. Don't look so worried. Everything is fine or I'd tell you. I do want this baby, and I'm taking care of myself."

"Okay. But you know you can call me at any time."

Andy stayed a few minutes longer and then left. All day he kept remembering the incident. When he didn't hear from Mary, he sighed with relief. His sister, after all, was a healthy woman, and her pregnancy agreed with her. Mary wasn't anything like his frail Allison. But it didn't stop him from worrying.

Katherine stood at the end of the library porch and looked at Andy's office building. It looked so . . . new. Rain and wind hadn't mellowed it yet. The shutters were white wood and not the ugly plastic ones she feared would be put on. The porch floorboards hadn't been stained and the flower boxes on the railing were empty. She and Mary were delegated to fill them with geraniums, petunias, and daisies this weekend. The forsythia bushes had already been planted at the foundation.

Mrs. Stone came to stand beside Katherine.

"Well, we did it, didn't we? The building does look Victorian and blends in well with the rest of the street."

Katherine nodded her head. "Andy was a good sport about changing his plans. I didn't think he would see things our way."

"He's a wonder. A local boy who made good." Mrs. Stone was lost in thought for a few minutes. "You know, since Andy has done so much, maybe we should name a street after him."

Katherine gave a hoot of laughter. "Mrs. Stone, don't be ridiculous. He'd hate it."

"I suppose you're right."

Two other society members came out of the restaurant and headed toward the library.

"Good afternoon," Katherine called to them.

"We're not coming in. We've just come to see the building," Mrs. Burman said. "I can't get over how nice it is."

"To think we were so worried about how it would turn out," Flora Edwards added.

"And we've had something interesting to look at all these weeks as well," Mrs. Stone said. "Everyone in town must have come this way, haven't they?"

"Yes. Sometimes they even come into the library," Katherine said with a laugh. "I've never been this busy in the summer before. I didn't get my addition, but the library has benefited."

Katherine waved good-bye as the women dispersed and entered the library. Her gaze was drawn to the window that overlooked the wall of Andy's building. She had loved looking out that window to the wetlands outside the village limits and seeing the birds soaring and flying in flocks. Sometimes, she even saw deer and wild turkeys. In the distance the Adirondack Mountains loomed against the blue sky. No longer would she see this ethereal sight from her window.

She felt Queenie brushing against her leg and picked her up. Queenie came with her to the library every day and was much loved and made over by the library pa-

79

trons. The children especially were delighted to see the cat each Thursday afternoon.

"She's very friendly," one of the smaller children said. "She likes me."

"Pet her as much as you like, only do it gently. You'll know if she's especially happy when she purrs loudly," Katherine said.

"She's purring now," came the delighted cry.

Making Katherine's job easier, it was simple then to go to the books on cats and kittens, as well as other animals. The construction next door also activated interest in buildings and architecture. In all, she was happier as a librarian this summer than she had ever been before. Seeing Andy every day added greatly to her happiness, of course!

"See you next week," she called out to the children.

Saturday afternoon at 1:00 Andy knocked on Katherine's back door.

"Andy, don't tell me that Mary's sick or something and can't come to her baby shower tonight," Katherine cried.

"She's fine, but she thought you might need some help with the streamers. She volunteered me."

"Wonderful. I hate to get up on ladders even if it's only two feet off the floor."

Andy's eyebrows rose. "What? My intrepid librarian is afraid of heights? How do you get those books up on the top shelves?"

"You've got me. I have a crew of tall boys to do it for

me. I know it's silly, but I fell off the top of a ladder when I was thirteen and never got over it," Katherine confessed.

"But for Mary you were going to be brave?"

"Well, I was going to call someone." She smiled at Andy. "Now I don't have to."

Katherine handed rolls of blue and white crepe paper to Andy. She wanted them to be just right, but he kept unfurling them or dropping them.

"Andrew Stratton, you fraud. Stop fooling around and do it right," she ordered.

Andy laughed. "I wondered how long it would take you to catch on. I helped to decorate the gym for the prom, and I haven't forgotten how to do it."

"You and Melissa were king and queen that year, weren't you?" Katherine remembered peeping in and seeing the crowning. She was too young to attend. Melissa was beautiful in a white and silver gown, and Andy was so handsome in a black tuxedo.

"Yeah, that was great. I had a good time in school."

Katherine felt a pang of sorrow. She hadn't had an active social life. She had concentrated on her studies and being president of the library club.

Katherine thanked Andy for doing the streamers.

"What else do you want me to do?"

"That's it. I have everything else organized. I got the party favors ready last night, and made the refreshments after that. I like to do everything ahead of time if possible."

She flushed under Andy's speculative gaze.

"Are you always so organized?" he asked.

Katherine's good spirits took a nosedive. She must appear like the world's dullest person to Andy.

"I'm sorry. I didn't mean it the way you took it. I could do with a course in organization right now. You'd be good for me." More and more, she was becoming necessary to his happiness.

He walked to the door.

"Thanks for all your help and your company. Tell Mary to be on time. That's all she has to do."

With Andy gone, the house felt empty. Katherine saw the hand of her friend in his appearance. Mary didn't care much for Franklin, and she praised Andy all the time. It would make her happy to have them get together. Oh, well. She had to get back to the shower preparations.

Katherine loved baby showers. As always, she looked forward with longing to the one that would be given for her someday. She only hoped it wouldn't be years from now—especially since Andy was back in town.

A week later the sun shined brightly, and a gentle breeze ruffled the leaves on the trees.

"I'd forgotten how exciting the Fourth of July used to be," Andy said to Katherine as he fell into step beside her. They walked toward the center of all the activity at the end of Main Street.

The parade had been at noon. The children spent the afternoon on the carnival rides and at the game booths of chance. The evening activities would be starting soon.

"The school band was a little off-key, don't you think, or am I being critical?" Andy asked.

Katherine smiled. "No, you're right. The kids don't take instrumental music as much as they did when we went to school."

"Everything changes with time," Andy said, a thoughtful note to his voice. He walked on with her silently.

"I hear your baby shower was a big success," he finally said. "You must have invited everyone in the village. What a load of gifts!" he said.

"Mary has lots of friends who are so happy she's having a baby. She and Burt would have been wonderful parents to an adopted child, but there's nothing like having your own baby. I'm so happy for her. I want to have one of my own so much."

"You have definite ideas on this baby thing, don't you?" Andy asked. "No chance of you changing them?"

Katherine shook her head. "No. On this I will never change unless a physical reason prevents it. Why do you ask?"

"Just curious."

She took his arm. "Let's not get so serious. We'll concentrate on having some fun."

They reached the amusement area. Katherine loved the old handmade, painted carousel. She knew that this was the last time it would come to the village. It was going to be placed in a museum in Florida.

"When was the last time you rode on the merry-go-round?" Katherine asked with a laugh.

"Right now. I'll even catch the ring for you."

When he almost fell off his horse catching the ring, she laughed.

"I take this for my thanks," he said and he kissed her.

"Oh," was all Katherine could manage in reply. She looked around to see who had seen this public display, but saw only the children lined up for their ride. She took the hand Andy held out to her as they crossed the street. She was so happy she didn't taste the hot dog with all the fixings that he bought for her.

"Did Portland have a big celebration on the Fourth of July?"

"A parade, of course, and fireworks at night. Pine View's way is unique. You have to only look around at the other villages and towns near us. They all come here because they don't do much in their area. I'm surprised I forgot this."

Andy's gaze became fixed on a distant cloud. Katherine had the sinking feeling she'd rekindled sad memories by mentioning his life in Oregon. After four years was Andy still grieving for Allison and his son? How deep his love for her must have been. She didn't want to believe it was a once-in-a-lifetime love, a love that could never be given to another woman in a different way.

There were many books written on that theme. Mr. Burgess, the hardware store owner, hadn't remarried for that reason.

"My Sadie," Mr. Burgess told Katherine once, "she was my life. No one can take her place."

So it could be true for Andy. She was always being foolish, wanting him against all odds. But if there were a chance with him, she'd never give up.

Looking up, she saw Melissa and Franklin coming over to them. Not what she wanted. She stood up when Andy did.

"Let's go to the bandstand for the concert," Franklin suggested. "If we go now, we'll get a good seat."

"A terrific idea," Andy said. He put his hand under Katherine's elbow, and she fell in step with him. Franklin and Melissa followed.

The four of them took seats in front of the white bandstand. To Katherine's surprise, Melissa took a seat on the other side of Andy and Franklin, next to her. There was nothing she could do about it, but she felt uncomfortable with the arrangement. It didn't look as though she was with Andy. Melissa immediately began to talk to Andy, and he turned to her.

As though on cue, Franklin asked, "Are you a cat owner again?"

"Queenie is mine. She's a big attraction at the library. Fortunately, I haven't had any complaints about her being there."

"It's good there are so many medications for allergies. I'm glad I'm not allergic to any animals."

Katherine remembered Andy holding Queenie. He too wasn't allergic to cats. A happy fact to remember.

When the concert started, they settled down to listen.

"Oh, dear," Katherine said with a quiet groan a few minutes later. The band again hit a few sour notes. "I'll have to give them credit for effort."

Katherine gave a sidelong glance to her left. Was Melissa trying to snuggle against Andy? It pleased Katherine to see he didn't put his arm around her shoulders. Instead, he looked straight ahead. Melissa gave him an exasperated look and sank back in her seat.

"Ooh!" exclaimed Katherine as a burst of fireworks lit up the sky after the concert ended. "What a wonderful ending to another Fourth of July, Pine View style!"

When she got ready for bed, Katherine hummed a strain from the musical, *Oklahoma*. The Fourth of July celebration this year had been as joyous as the opening song because she was with Andy.

If only she and Andy had been at the concert together on a real date, sitting side by side, with his arm drawing her close to him. In the dark, who knew what Andy might have whispered to her or the kisses they would have exchanged if they hadn't had company!

No harm in dreaming . . .

Chapter Eight

"Come and see the interior of my building," Andy said to Katherine the next day. "You haven't been inside yet. Why?"

Katherine's cheeks flushed pink. Although many of the villagers had been in and out, she had waited to be asked to do so. It was as though she needed a personal invitation to come into Andy's special place.

"I didn't want to get in the way. But I'd like to see it."

Andy took her arm and walked her to the double oak doors of his building. On a gold plaque was the name of the company and its discrete computer logo. As she entered the foyer, Katherine felt a surge of pride and joy for Andy's success.

She glanced to the right and saw that the window was opposite the one in the library. She thought of how easy it would be to connect the two buildings. What a foolish thought. There was no practical reason for such a connection—except her constant desire to see Andy during the day whenever she wanted to!

"This is going to be a pleasant place to work in," she said after the tour of the first floor. "You and your architect have thought of everything."

Andy's face lit up like a Christmas tree. He smiled broadly. "Thanks. I'm glad you like it. Sometimes what's on paper isn't as good in reality, but I've been lucky. This is what I wanted. Care to see the upstairs?"

"Yes, and also the widow's walk if it's finished."

Katherine started walking up the wide stairway.

"There's an elevator—"

"No, thanks. I'd rather walk."

Katherine's hand grasped the smooth stair rail. She could easily imagine a blond boy sliding gleefully down the railing. That the boy looked like a young Andy was no surprise to her. A smile wreathed her lips at the thought.

"Why the smile?" Andy asked.

"Oh, only a happy thought about future days in this building."

"I hope the future will always be happy," Andy said thoughtfully.

The rooms on the second floor were as large and well designed as the ones downstairs. Katherine wondered about the size of the building. Would his business need so much space? The downstairs seemed more than adequate. But then, what did she know about Andy's plans for expansion in the future? He certainly had potential and so did his building.

When Katherine entered the widow's walk, she gasped. Before her, in all directions, the spectacular panorama of fields, mountains, and lakes went on and on as far as the eye could see.

"How beautiful," she exclaimed. "What a sight."

She turned to Andy and became aware he was only looking at her. Her breath caught and she felt weightless with delight.

"You'll have to conduct daily tours up here," she said as calmly as she could.

"Not on your life," Andy said. "This is a business building, not a tourist attraction. My employees can come here in their free time but no one else." He smiled. "Well, you can come anytime."

Katherine felt her face get warm at his invitation. She wondered what it would be like to be up here on a moonlit night with Andy's arms around her as she leaned against him. To turn away from the silver landscape so he could kiss her until the world was lost to her.

"Katherine . . . where did you go?" Andy asked. "You should have taken me with you!" he joked.

Katherine turned away in confusion. She took a deep breath and turned back to him. "I . . . that is, the view . . . is beyond words."

Andy laughed. She was grateful he didn't press the issue.

"Thanks for the tour," she said. "You should be very proud of this building."

Katherine walked slowly down the stairs. "When will you begin hiring?"

"I'll be taking applications starting next week. The office staff will get to work soon. Then we'll hire people for the manufacturing end."

"I see the foundation for your factory is almost finished. Because of the dip in the ground and the trees, we won't see much of it from the street," Katherine said.

Andy chuckled. "Guess your society won't be reading me the riot act about it having to look Victorian."

Katherine laughed with him, but she felt guilty. She had been wondering about how incongruous it was to have a factory building in their tree-lined, picturesque village. How fortunate that Andy had been able to purchase all the land he needed extending to the next street. Even the parking lot would be big enough for those who didn't want to walk to work or lived out of the village.

"I'll let you get back to work," Katherine said after they walked outside. "Thanks again for the tour."

"When it's finished, we'll tour the factory," he promised. "Just the two of us." Andy bent down and kissed her. When they pulled apart, his sweet smile and his words excited her. "You made me happy today," he said. "I'd like to spend the rest of the day with you, but it's impossible. I'll be in touch."

He quickly walked away from her and disappeared down the path leading to the factory site.

He left her speechless and bemused. His actions bewildered her. Was the kiss serious or just a friendly peck? Was he sorry to leave her? If only he would let her know how he really felt about her—talk to her. His actions tantalized her and made her long for words of love.

Katherine and two other members of the preservation society were having lunch the next day. As always these days, Andy was one of the topics of discussion.

"That Andy Stratton. I'm so happy he's so successful," Mrs. Furman said.

"What about the kids in your high school class, Katherine? How are they doing these days?" Mrs. Stone asked.

"Those who worked hard for good grades tend to do the same in the work force. However, so many have moved away because there's so little work in Pine View." She smiled. "I'm one of the lucky ones to find a job I love in my hometown."

"We're fortunate to have you," Mrs. Stone said loyally. "Now Andy has come back to help the village."

There was silence in the booth.

"There's Melissa Perry too," Mrs. Stone said. "I wonder what her plans are." She laughed. "Do you think she'll find husband number three here?"

Katherine's heart missed a beat. Husband number three? Could it be Andy? Surely not . . .

Katherine smiled. "Melissa is working at the bank. She's doing well, according to Franklin."

Mrs. Stone wasn't to be sidetracked. "She and Andy went together in high school. Seems they're a likely couple again especially since they're both so successful."

"I wouldn't know about that. But I do have to get back to the library. At least the worst of the construction noise is over."

Katherine smiled, said her good-byes, and left, eager to get away. She didn't want to be told what a perfect couple Andy and Melissa were. Though she had to agree, it didn't make it any easier for her.

Nor did seeing Andy and Melissa walking out of his building and coming toward her.

"Hi, got some great news," Andy said, "Melissa is going to be my business manager. Isn't that perfect?"

"Wonderful," Katherine said. She turned to Melissa. "I recall business was your major in college. Congratulations on your new job. You'll be a big help to Andy."

"Thanks. I'm happy I came back to Pine View. However, I only expected to work in the bank with Franklin. This is more challenging and interesting."

"When do you start?"

"In three days," Andy answered. "Melissa needs to work on the job applications. Fortunately, things are slow at the bank so she won't be leaving her brother in a lurch."

"Then we women will be seeing a lot of each other since we'll be working side by side—in a matter of speaking." Katherine turned toward the library. "See you both later. Bye for now."

The Wedding Cake

Katherine walked into the library, glad to stop smiling. Everyone's speculations about Melissa and Andy appeared to be coming true. And it didn't make her want to shout for joy.

At a restaurant the next day at noon, Katherine looked up as Franklin slid into the booth seat across from her.

"Looks good," he said watching her bite into a thick roast beef sandwich.

Katherine chewed a piece of bread and waited for Franklin to say why he was here. His black hair was windblown and he had loosened his tie. He wasn't his impeccable self. She speculated Franklin had a hard time this morning at the bank.

"Have you had lunch? Why don't you join me?" Katherine asked.

"I'll eat later. I came because I'd like to take you to dinner and the movies on Saturday night," he said. "Please," he added quickly.

Katherine knew she had to refuse. She wanted to go out only with Andy. Although she had gone out with Franklin on occasion before Andy's return, she didn't plan to do so anymore.

"Sorry, but I have other plans for Saturday."

After Franklin left, Katherine took her time finishing her lunch. She had no plans for Saturday. Why didn't she just tell Franklin she didn't want to go out with him? She didn't want to hurt him. She sighed. It was so hard to know what to do all the time.

"What's wrong with your world?" Andy asked as he took the seat vacated by Franklin. He smiled and his gaze was warm.

A sudden rush of pleasure filled Katherine. It was always like that when Andy came near her.

"Everything's fine," she said. *Since you're here*, she thought.

"Didn't look that way to me. Glad I caught you," Andy said. "How about going to dinner and dancing Saturday night? I had a good time the other night and hope you did too."

Katherine smothered a groan of disappointment. If only he had come before Franklin.

"Sorry, I can't."

"Going out with Franklin?"

"No. Does it matter to you?" she asked, hoping against hope.

"Sorry, I didn't mean to get personal." He stood up. "We'll get together another time, okay?"

"Sure. Another time."

Katherine finished her lunch, not tasting any of it. Why hadn't Andy shown more disappointment? He should have. Resentment simmered in her.

She left the restaurant with the determination to go back to work and not think of either of these men. She didn't need these hassles in her life.

On Saturday night Katherine watched TV and tried to read a book. The time passed very slowly. She had done this to herself. At 11:00 she went out to her patio and let the quiet of the evening seep into her lonely soul. The stars winked at her and cheered her spirits. This was what she needed. Men! Why did she bother?

She raised her arms to the sky and proclaimed, "Tonight, oh, Universe, I intend to take complete charge of my life, to do what I want, when I want to do it. My thoughts and my desires will create my reality—not the men in my life."

On Monday morning the rain ran down the windows of the library and obscured the view. Katherine didn't feel like smiling. Her chant to the heavens Saturday night had carried her through Sunday. Today, however, it wasn't so easy to follow her intentions.

She put aside all thoughts of Franklin and Andy. Facing her was the job of setting up a book-signing event for the book, *The Art of Fly Tying*, by Jeffrey Olson. Many in the village would turn up to show support because they were proud of Jeffrey's accomplishment. After all, not many retirees wrote and published a book at the age of seventy-nine.

Queenie brushed up against her leg and Katherine picked her up. "Queenie, it's a dismal day. We aren't going to have much company," she said. She closed her eyes and rubbed her cheek against Queenie's soft head.

"Things have come to a sad state when a beautiful woman has only a cat to talk to."

Andy's voice startled Katherine. She hugged Queenie so hard the cat gave a yowl and leaped out of her arms. The cat arched her back and swished her tail,. She jumped on the couch and curled into a ball.

"Will you stop that? You're always sneaking up on me," Katherine complained.

"Sorry," Andy said but his grin was firmly in place. "I wanted to see you before anyone else did."

Katherine had an idea whom he meant, yet her traitorous heart was ready to forget her determination to not see Andy either. When it came to Andy, she was willing to forgive.

"I'm always happy to see you," she said and she smiled up at him. Impulsively, she fluttered her lashes briefly—just enough to make Andy raise his eyebrows and grin. She quickly turned away from him and seated herself at the desk.

"What can I do for you?"

"Come with me to the baseball game at Hawkins Stadium in Bradford. Wednesday is your afternoon off, isn't it?"

"That could be fun. Yes, I'll go with you."

"That's great. We'll leave at one o'clock if it's okay with you."

Andy reached over and kissed her, a light and tender kiss, an undemanding kiss. He smiled at her gasp.

"Have to get back to work," he said. "See you later."

Andy's light kiss felt like a firebrand. She wanted to think he had made her his! Katherine went about her work in a daze of wonder and delight. Another kiss from Andy. This was a habit she wanted to become permanent.

Though the rain continued and a stiff wind was playing havoc with umbrellas, Franklin came at 3:00. He had parked his car in front and dashed into the library. His black hair glistened from the raindrops.

"This is hardly a day for a chat," Katherine said. She handed him several tissues to dry his face.

"Will you go with me to the school concert Friday night? I know the band isn't the best, but we need to support the school activities."

"Can I give you my answer on Thursday?"

"That's fine with me."

"Good-bye, Franklin. I'll let you know."

After Franklin left, Katherine wandered aimlessly about the library before she returned books to the shelves. She wished Andy had asked her to the concert. Since Franklin had asked first, she'd go with him as she had last year.

Because of the rain, no patrons came. The library was so quiet. The old stories about the house being haunted came to mind on such dark, dismal days. The spirits of long dead occupants were supposed to walk around.

On this desolate day, her imagination could easily play tricks on her. She wished some readers would come trooping in and keep her company. Even Queenie had deserted her.

Since it was time to write an article for the village newsletter, Katherine turned to the section on the Anderson family in the county history. They had built this house in 1853, and it stayed in the family for years. The last descendent deeded the house to the village with the request that it be turned into the village library. Katherine again gave silent thanks that this had happened. She did so love the old house and being able to work in it.

Chapter Nine

Wednesday was a perfect baseball day.

"I'm glad the Bradford city council enticed a minor league baseball team to come here," Katherine said. "And to print a program."

Katherine fished in her purse and pulled out a pencil.

"Why the pencil?" Andy's folded program was in his back pocket.

"I like to keep score—every hit, run, error, and everything else. That's the only way the game holds my interest."

"That's ridiculous. Just watch the game."

Katherine smiled at him and kept her program open on her lap.

Andy had thought Katherine might be bored today, but not this. What fun was it to watch baseball played if all you did was record it? Allison had loved the game and was as excited as he had been over the plays.

Andy looked at Katherine.

She had on a pink summer blouse with a printed flower on it, white slacks, and sandals. A pink baseball hat perched on her brown curls. She didn't look like a librarian, but with her program open and the pencil poised over the page, she acted like one. He would have to get Katherine to lighten up and enjoy life.

No, she wasn't like Allison . . .

Suddenly, Andy experienced an epiphany. He had just compared Katherine to Allison without a pang of grief or loss. After four years he had healed his broken heart and was ready to grant Allison's last request. He no longer thought of Katherine only as his sister's best friend—not when his heart beat faster every time he saw her and touched her. And their kisses were something else!

Lost in thought, Andy missed seeing the first error. Katherine didn't. And so it went for several innings. She didn't miss a play or recording it.

By the fourth inning, Andy had had enough.

"Katherine," Andy's voice rose in irritation, "Put that pencil down and just watch the game." He wanted her to pay attention to him and talk to him—not just write in the program.

Katherine smiled at him so sweetly that his heart gave a flip. It would have been so easy to give into temptation and kiss her.

"You watch the game your way, and I'll do it my

way." She looked back at the field. "Another error," she said. "Our team isn't doing well. I'd like to see at least one homerun."

Katherine ignored the dark look Andy leveled at her. She enjoyed teasing Andy. She remembered her dad taking her to her first professional game. He started her keeping score on the program in order to learn the game. Since then, she just did it that way. Baseball wasn't her favorite sport, and she tended to get bored unless she did the program thing.

Katherine's thoughts wandered away from the game. She enjoyed going out with Andy and having fun. She hoped with all her heart this was the beginning of many such occasions.

"You missed that strike," Andy said to her.

"Oh, so I did." She wrote it in. From then on Katherine kept her attention on the game, or Andy's reminders rang in her ears.

"Sorry you were bored today," Andy said after the game. He opened the car door and waited until she fastened her seat belt.

"I wasn't bored," Katherine protested.

"Yeah, sure." Andy's reply was surly.

"I had a very enjoyable afternoon. I wanted to see the new stadium. Going to the game brought back many happy memories with my father. Thank you for taking me today."

"Always happy to please you."

Katherine took comfort in his reply. It seemed that it didn't take much for Andy to want to please her.

During the ride home, Katherine encouraged Andy to talk about his life working in the computer field. It made her feel close to him, to be able to visualize him at his work. She steered clear of asking questions about his personal life. She wondered if she would ever be at ease with thoughts of Andy having an intimate life with another woman. If they married, would he be comparing the two marriages most of the time? That thought scared her. She had to bury it right away.

At her door she said, "I'm going to make my prize sparerib dinner on Sunday. Please come and share it with me," she said.

"Spareribs? One of my favorites," Andy said, a ready grin on his lips. "What time?"

"Come at five." Katherine smiled. Ah, she hoped the old adage of food and men still applied—not for lack of trying on her part.

Friday evening Katherine and Franklin walked into the central school for the band concert.

"Want to sit in the balcony?" Franklin asked. A smile curved his lips, and his black eyebrows were raised.

Katherine laughed. "No, thank you. Sound rises, doesn't it? I don't think I could take it. Let's sit here, on the side."

Parents, friends, and some tourists filled the auditorium. School functions were always supported enthusiastically. Katherine had always been proud of that. She often thought Pine View was an example of a Norman

Rockwell place—almost too good to be true, but nevertheless, her village and her home.

Before she sat down, Katherine scanned the auditorium. She smiled and waved to her friends. On the far side she spotted Mr. and Mrs. Stratton. Andy sat beside his mother. Katherine quickly sat down, not wanting to appear as though she was looking for him. She had a feeling Andy had seen her with Franklin. His scowl might have been her clue. She hadn't told him about coming with Franklin. Well, Andy should have asked her.

Katherine dropped into her seat, feeling her cheeks flame. She looked up into Franklin's admiring gaze.

His gaze took in the high color in her smooth cheeks. "You're beautiful tonight," he said.

"Thank you."

"You're wearing the green dress I've always thought did you justice."

Katherine gave a gasp of surprise. She hadn't thought Franklin would remember the dress. She felt better when he said more.

"And you look even lovelier in it this time."

"Thank you, Franklin." His compliment made her uneasy. It wasn't like Franklin at all. "Do you have a photographic memory?"

Franklin laughed. "Don't I wish. No, I just remember all our times together."

She didn't remember them. Why was Franklin telling her this tonight? It wasn't even a romantic setting. Was Franklin still competing with Andy? Oh, she didn't want this.

The concert started, and Katherine tried to listen. Unfortunately, her thoughts tormented her. She was twenty-eight and still single. Since her first year of college, she had had any number of dates and friendships. None had become serious. Was it because she was the one who put the brakes on?

Had the wedding cake episode indirectly sabotaged her life? Andy had been the love and obsession of her life from childhood. He had tolerated her young devotion. When she put the wedding cake under her pillow, she had been at a very impressionable age. It was what she wanted with all her heart. That it would happen she believed without question. Again, a belief—not a fact. Since Andy said he would wait for her to grow up, she counted on it. How she longed to grow up in a hurry.

But he hadn't waited.

He had married. Yes, married another woman.

Had she subconsciously come to believe if she couldn't have Andy she didn't want any other man? It could well be true.

Then Allison died. Four years passed before Andy came home. Her hope had revived, only to find Andy still grieved for his wife and son. He also dated Melissa.

Katherine sighed.

"Yes, they are pretty bad, aren't they?" Franklin said.

That Franklin had misinterpreted the cause of the sigh was a relief to Katherine. "That's true, but I'm still glad we came. I love these kids. They try so hard."

"You should have some of your own," Franklin said, his gaze intent.

"Someday." Katherine shrugged her shoulders. "Plenty of time yet. I have to find my man."

"You don't have to look far," Franklin said fervently, "I'm right here."

Katherine gasped and resisted a hysterical desire to laugh. "Franklin, this isn't the place or the time for such a serious declaration. I can't believe you've said this!"

She saw the blush that colored his face and his agonized look. This was a Franklin who was also astonished at his own behavior. She felt it best not to comment further. She kept her attention on the band.

At last, the final note of the music died away.

Katherine rose, and they wended their way to the back of the auditorium.

"You didn't give me an answer," Franklin persisted.

Katherine shook her head. "Because you shouldn't have said that. We are only friends, remember."

Goodness, she wanted to be married, but not to Franklin. She should have known better than to go out with him again. Only it was so hard to say no to an old friend.

At sunset on Sunday, Katherine glanced at her wristwatch. She looked across the lawn to the white fence that separated their two yards. The gate had a white trellis covered with morning glory vines. On the dot, Andy came through the gate from his house. He waved to Katherine, and she waved back. Her heartbeat accelerated, and her mouth became dry. It was always like this. Today, even more so.

Since the temperature was in the middle eighties, Andy had on a pair of Bermuda shorts and a white sleeveless T-shirt. He was tanned a deep bronze, and his muscles rippled as he walked toward her.

Katherine couldn't catch her breath. Her desires made her want to fling herself into his arms. It was a good thing she was on her patio with a sturdy railing penning her in. She turned her back to him in order to tend to the spareribs on the new grill.

"Mmm, smells good," Andy said. He stood close behind her. His breath was soft and warm on her cheek. If only she felt free to lean back and have his arms enfold her. A heavenly thought.

"Hey, I think something is burning," Andy warned. He took her hand and helped her turn over the rib.

Katherine gave a shaky laugh. She brushed the ribs with sauce and turned them over.

"Would you like something to drink? I made fresh lemonade. It's on the table."

When Andy moved away, Katherine took a deep breath. Why couldn't she control her physical reaction to Andy? They were neighbors and friends and nothing more. Yet he kissed her and asked her out. It was hard to not hope and dream their relationship would develop and ultimately bring her happiness.

A whiff of charred rib and Andy's laughter jerked her back into the present.

"I don't know, Katherine, if I can count on having dinner with you tonight," he teased.

"Don't worry. I've finally found the temperature setting. This is the first time I've used this grill."

"Sure, sure. Why not let me do the grilling?"

"All right. You take over and I'll finish putting out the rest of the dinner." She held out her frilly apron to him. "Do you need this?"

Andy's raised eyebrows were his answer. Katherine thought it would have made a humorous picture for her album.

Dinner was a leisurely affair. By unspoken agreement, the conversation, though spirited at times, was on impersonal topics. They ignored all mention of the band concert. The movie they had seen was a safe subject.

"I loved seeing *The Scarlet Pimpernel*. What other classics will be shown soon?"

"I'll have Mary look them up." Andy's grin was sheepish. "She's the person who told me to take you to it."

Katherine's hoot of laughter took away any of Andy's fears of displeasure.

"I just knew you had help. What kind of movies do you go to?"

Andy launched into a list and a brief synopsis of some of them. From movies they went on to share opposite views on political talk shows on TV.

"Wow, you're very definite about your political views," he said.

Katherine tossed her hair over her shoulder. "Yes, I want to see some positive changes, and this administration has to get back in touch with the people." She gave a rueful smile. "Don't mind me. This is still the best country in the world and I'm glad I'm living during this accelerated time period. I look forward to see all the wonderful changes that are coming."

"I agree with you there," Andy said. He grinned. "To get down to something really important. May I have another cup of coffee?"

Katherine laughed with him and complied. Andy backed up his words of praise of her cooking by taking second helpings. Katherine accepted his offer to clear the table and wash up what didn't go into the dishwasher.

"You've done this before," she said.

"You forget I've been on my own for four years." He grinned. "Must admit I've enjoyed Mom's spoiling me. She won't let me do anything."

Katherine was relieved Andy talked easily about the years since Allison died. Four years was a long time, but still . . .

She pulled forward two deck chairs so they faced the East. She knew that the full moon would be rising soon, and she loved watching its slow progress upward in the sky.

"I've searched on the Internet about computer chips, but I still don't have a clear picture of what you will be doing."

"Computer chips are in many products. I'm concentrating on making those to be used in medical equipment. Since my company is small, I have to specialize. This kind of manufacturing is different in that so much time each day has to be spent in keeping the workers and the factory dust and dirt free." Andy grinned. "Because of their outfits, you'll think people you know are going to outer space instead of to a workbench."

"How interesting. You'll have a tour of the facilities on opening day, won't you?"

"Sure, but I'm giving you a personal one before that."

"I'd like that. I warn you, I'll ask a lot of questions."

"No problem. I'll probably bore you with all my information. I eat and live computer work."

Katherine smiled at Andy. His eyes sparkled and a glow of pride surrounded him. She reached over and patted his arm. His big hand covered hers, and he gave hers a squeeze.

"You've come a long way, Andy. I'm so proud of you."

"The credit goes to Allison. She was the driving force in my life," Andy said. "As you remember, I was only interested in sports and girls in high school."

"She must have been a remarkable person."

"Yes."

Katherine waited for Andy to say more. Seeing the bleak look which filled his eyes, she was at a loss for words. For Andy, Allison's death was still a present pain. A feeling of despair filled Katherine. Andy wasn't ready for a relationship with another woman at this time—perhaps never. Did he want only a pleasant evening of casual enjoyment with her? But surely the kisses and touches must be leading to a deeper relationship. Andy would never just lead her on. She couldn't be mistaken about her assessment of Andy's character.

Andy broke the silence.

"When I took my first computer course, I met Allison. She took pity on me and helped me get started. For me, it was love at first sight." Andy laughed. "It took a lot of convincing on my part to prove to her I was dead serious about my feelings for her."

"When did you marry?"

"A year after we met. Allison wanted to have a baby right away, but I wanted to wait. Besides, Allison, physically, wasn't the strongest person in the world, no matter how she tried to deny it. The doctor thought all was okay, and that was all the encouragement she needed. When she finally became pregnant, she was so happy." Andy stared out over the garden.

"Were you happy about having a baby too?" Katherine had to know. The birth of a baby had to be a shared joy.

"Sure. It was great. I had a good salary, and we had bought a nice little house. We painted the nursery yellow. Allison put Mother Goose decals on the walls."

"You don't have to tell me what happened, Andy."

"I can talk about it now," Andy said. "Everything was fine until the seventh month. Allison went into early labor that went on and on. It was a breech birth with all kinds of complications. The doctors did the best they

110

could. Allison lived for two more days after the baby was born. My son Jeffrey died three days later. He was so small, and he had heart damage. He just didn't have a chance."

Katherine wanted to put her arms around Andy, to comfort him. She felt like she could cry for a long time over the tragedy. She saw that Andy was calm and dry-eyed. It was only when she saw his clenched fists that she knew telling the story wasn't easy for him.

"At least Allison was able to hold her beloved baby in her arms. She never knew about his problems. She was so happy. When she held him and kissed him, there was a radiance about her."

"I'm so sorry. Please don't tell me any more. I don't need to know," she said.

Andy shook his head and looked at her. It was as though he realized that he had gone away in the telling and now came back to her.

Katherine took a deep breath. Before she could change the conversation, Andy surprised her.

"Allison made me promise to remarry, so our son would have a mother, and I wouldn't be alone." Andy's smile was sweet and so sad. "Of course I promised. It's hard to realize that four years have gone by. I've become pretty set in my ways and expectations. I'm not sure another woman would put up with me or go along with my wishes."

"You're being too hard on yourself," Katherine protested.

It was as she had thought. The wedding cake dream

was dead in the water. Or was it? It did sound as though Andy was considering carrying out his promise. He needed time, and she was willing to wait. She certainly had had lots of experience doing that.

"Would you like some more coffee?" Katherine asked. "I made a chocolate cake too."

"No, thanks. I'll take a rain check on the cake. Think I'll get back home."

He went to Katherine and took her hands in his. "Dinner was great. Thanks."

He bent down and kissed her cheek. It was a kiss like the brush of a butterfly's wings.

"Good night, Andy," she said, hiding the ache she felt at his sweet kiss. "We'll do this again."

She watched him stride across the lawn and through the gate. For once, no merry whistle came from Andy. She wondered if he was sorry to have opened up to her, to tell her about Allison. She knew from experience that personal confessions caused a strain in a friendship that often never healed. Then again, talking helped to heal. Which would it do for Andy?

While Katherine stayed out on the patio and watched the moon rise in the sky, she pondered the events of her dinner with Andy. It had enlightened her about Andy's past life. At least she knew Andy thought of carrying out his wife's promise to remarry.

Suddenly, irrational hope blossomed in her. Wouldn't it be wonderful if, oh, if her wedding cake dream came true after all!

Chapter Ten

At 7:00 on Saturday evening Katherine opened the door.

"Come in, Franklin. I have to run upstairs for my evening bag."

Franklin had come to her a few days ago. "Katherine, please go with me to the Banker's Ball. We had a good time last year." Seeing her hesitation he said, "For old times' sake."

Katherine was torn with doubt. "I'll go with you, but only as a friend, and not on a date."

"Fine with me."

She hoped Franklin would be honored this year. He had worked hard to revamp the village bank and had opened a branch in Bradford. Franklin was a go-getter. She appreciated his good qualities.

Katherine looked at Franklin. The superb tailoring

113

of his dinner jacket fitted smoothly across his broad shoulders. His black hair was cut short, a conservative styling that suited his profession. She noticed the speculative and approving glances some women gave Franklin. It happened every time she went out with Franklin. She hadn't paid attention to this before. There was no doubt that Franklin was an eligible man.

"Good. I'm glad our table is near the front," Franklin said and seated Katherine. "You're so beautiful tonight. That gown suits you. There isn't a woman here who outshines you."

Katherine felt her cheeks grow warm from his praise. She had chosen a simple white sheath. The neckline was lower than she usually wore, but she liked the row of rhinestones around it. It was worth the fortune she spent on it.

When Franklin seated her, his hand lightly caressed her shoulders. Katherine knew immediately that his touch didn't thrill her as Andy's did. In fact, all she felt for Franklin was friendship. She had to make Franklin believe that. Had she been giving him the wrong signals by going out with him, again and again—especially tonight?

The awards ceremony started after the dinner. At last, the master of ceremonies came to the most important part of the program as far as Katherine was concerned.

"We're happy to announce that Franklin Perry of Pine View is the recipient of the Banker of the Year award."

For several seconds Franklin stayed in his seat. He

looked as though he was having a hard time believing this was true.

"Come on up, Franklin," the master of ceremonies urged, "It's true." His laughter joined others amid the clapping and cheers.

"Go up, Franklin. I'm so happy for you," Katherine said.

Franklin sprang to his feet and went to the stage. Katherine was glad to be there to see this crowning moment of his career.

They danced for the rest of the evening.

Katherine enjoyed the dancing. Franklin would burst out with an exclamation about his award and twirl her with exuberance. Katherine laughed and celebrated with him. When the thought of Andy intruded, she quickly banished it away. Tonight belonged to Franklin, her friend.

When Franklin pulled into the rest area overlooking the valley, unease raced through her veins. Though there was no moon, the stars were many and very bright. Below them, a row of street lights were orange blobs along the main street of Singleton.

"Shall we?" Franklin asked.

Katherine unhooked her seat belt. She waited for him to come around and open her door. The night was warm and a soft breeze caressed her.

Franklin put his hand below her elbow and guided her to the rock wall that lined the cliff's edge. He stood close to her.

Katherine kept a breathless silence. She waited for

Franklin to speak, afraid of her premonition—not wanting to hear the question he might ask.

"Katherine, will you marry me? I've cared for you for a long time, but I didn't feel I was ready." He gave a short, triumphant laugh. "Getting the award tonight made me confident."

His head began to tilt down, and she realized he was going to kiss her. She turned her head away, and his lips brushed her cheek.

"Please say yes," Franklin urged.

"This sounds Victorian," she laughed a little wildly, "but this is so sudden. You've taken me by surprise."

"Surely you've known I loved you and wanted to marry you."

"You never said it," Katherine protested. "I'm not a mind reader."

"We've been dating for three years." Franklin's voice had an edge to it.

"No we haven't! We've only been going together out of convenience."

Katherine fought for control. She was furious for being so blind. She had put herself in this position.

Franklin interrupted her thoughts. "I'm waiting for my answer." He started to put his arms around her.

Katherine pushed him away. Emotion made her tremble.

"I don't love you!" she almost shouted. She took a deep breath and said more quietly, "I admire you, and I enjoy your company, but since I don't love you, I can't marry you."

Franklin gave a bitter laugh. "I thought you cared for me, or why else would you keep going out with me? Have you been stringing me along while you waited for Andy to come back?"

"Andy? Of course not!" Katherine's voice rose an octave. "Andy doesn't come into the picture."

Katherine walked quickly to the car, got in, and fastened her seat belt.

Franklin slid into his seat. He turned to her and grasped her hand.

"I'm sorry this came as such a surprise."

Katherine slowly drew her hand away. Franklin's plea touched her heart, but it didn't change the situation.

"Franklin, I care for you as a friend, but I can't marry you."

Katherine's eyes filled with tears. This was so hard.

"At least you got your fabulous award, if not the girl," she joked, giving him a shaky smile.

Franklin rose to the occasion. "You're right, Katherine darling. I'm glad you were there with me."

He started the car.

"And I'll keep working on the girl," he promised.

"I've asked you twice for my book," Mrs. Stone complained on Monday morning.

Katherine started in dismay. "I'm sorry but I was thinking of . . . of . . . a problem."

Since the award ceremony, she thought of Franklin's proposal often. It still took her by surprise. Yet she should have seen it coming. She had laughed off his remark at the school concert. In all probability, if Andy hadn't returned, She and Franklin would have continued going out together until she accepted a proposal of marriage.

When she told him she didn't love him but did have affection for him, she was being honest. He didn't thrill her or quicken her heartbeat. She didn't long to see him again the minute he left her.

But . . .

He was steady, reliable, and dependable. He was easy to be with and as comfortable as an old shoe. His winning smile was sweet. He would be a faithful husband and a good father. These were attributes any woman could always rely on. And, in time, come to love him, surely and deeply.

But not her. She was in love with Andy.

Andy.

Tall, blond, and handsome. A ready smile activating the deep dimple in his left cheek and a great sense of humor. Even a successful businessman. A very eligible man.

And she loved him.

That was the most important of all arguments for marriage. She wondered about the deathbed promise his wife asked of him. Was he waiting to fall in love again before he did so? If so, were his kisses and attention helping him to decide if she was the one? Oh, why couldn't he just love her immediately and know it? She didn't want to have to wait any longer.

Katherine sighed. She had no power over Andy's feelings or actions.

When the door opened and Melissa came breezing in, she welcomed the visit. Melissa, having started her job, often dropped in during her lunch hour or coffee break. Katherine tried to warm up to her, but found it difficult. They were so different in every way. It didn't help that Melissa dressed like a model. Katherine often felt dowdy beside her. She wondered if Andy ever made a comparison and, if so, what was the result? She didn't want to know.

"Wasn't that wonderful for Franklin to get the banking award? If I had had any idea it was going to happen, I would have gone to the ball with Andy. He would have taken me."

Katherine was glad Melissa hadn't gone, especially with Andy. A sudden, troubling thought occurred. If she accepted Franklin's proposal, it would make Melissa her sister-in-law. Such a thought was a little daunting. Melissa's next statement made it even more so.

"Wouldn't it be perfect if you marry Franklin, and I get Andy to propose? We could have a double wedding!"

"Andy and you are getting married?" Katherine's voice rose in surprise. Dismay swamped her, and her heart thundered in her chest.

Melissa laughed. "He hasn't asked me yet, but I'm working on it."

The smug look on Melissa's face showed her confidence. Katherine knew how determined Melissa could become and how she usually got what she wanted.

Katherine said quickly, "But I haven't accepted Franklin's proposal. He took me by surprise—"

"Oh, you'll say yes when you think some more. After all, Franklin's a great catch, and you can't do better."

Katherine was annoyed. "Melissa, you're wrong. I agree Franklin is a wonderful man, but I'm not in love with him." She frowned. "Please don't go to Franklin with your ideas. It's really none of your business. Let us make our own decisions."

"Okay, I'll be good." Melissa smiled.

Katherine didn't trust the promise or the smile.

While busy checking in books and getting them on the shelves, Katherine thought how complicated her life was becoming.

Franklin tried calling her every night, but she put a stop to that.

Months ago Franklin talked about what he wanted in a wife. At that time, she noted that loving the woman was just one of the requirements. She couldn't remember if it was the most important one.

Franklin would make a good husband for some woman other than herself. She wasn't going to settle for second best. She wanted and was going to hold out for the whole romantic love story. She couldn't help it if her traitorous heart kept longing for Andy—that he would be the one to make her love story come true.

The sudden crash of thunder and the flash of lightning made her jump. The rain pounded on the porch roof.

She grabbed Queenie and hugged her. "I should have driven to work this morning. I don't even have an umbrella with me. Why didn't I believe the weather report? We'll have to wait until the rain stops before we walk home."

The door of the library opened and a gust of wind came in. To Katherine's surprise and delight, Andy entered. Giving it a shake, he closed his big black umbrella. Katherine smiled. She couldn't have conjured up a more welcome person to rescue her from the elements.

"What a storm! I didn't see your car so you must have walked this morning. I'll take you home. My car's outside and," he laughed, "Mother made me take this umbrella with me."

"Mothers always know best!" Katherine said. "I'll gladly let you take us home. Fortunately, I have Queenie's carrier with me. She definitely doesn't like to get wet."

Under the umbrella, Andy held her close to his side until they reached the car. This unexpected chance to be with Andy made happiness sing in Katherine's heart. Before she got in the car, she looked into his face, a smile on her lips.

Andy did exactly what she longed for—he kissed her. A kiss that stole away her breath. A very satisfying kiss. A very lover-like kiss.

The rain pounded on the umbrella and made a puddle

at their feet. The magical moment had to end. With a happy laugh, Katherine got in the car.

As quickly as it came, the storm departed. By the time they arrived at Katherine's house, the rain stopped. Andy carried Queenie into the house and let her out.

"Thank you for bringing us home," Katherine said with the memory of their kiss still thrilling her. "Won't you stay? I can make us something to eat."

"I'd like nothing better, but Mother's expecting me. I really want to stay, but I can't tonight."

He pulled her close to him and kissed her. "I'll take a rain check for now. Don't forget to ask me at a more convenient time."

After Andy left, Katherine recalled the kisses again and again. They were becoming a regular occurrence, and she couldn't be happier. Surely they meant as much to Andy as they did to her. Though no commitment in words had been made, the kisses spoke their own language. The words would come; she had no doubts about it.

To fill her evening, she crocheted an afghan for Mary's baby. While her fingers flew, she dreamed of having her own baby. She didn't stop at one. Hers wouldn't suffer from loneliness as she had.

The next day, Katherine helped Mary shop for baby furniture. It took hours because there was so much to choose from and decisions to be made. It would be delivered in three days.

Back at Mary's house, they went into the nursery.

"I love the western theme," Katherine said. "I'm not sure I'd want to know the sex of my baby. There's something exciting about not knowing what it would be."

"I know what you mean. I had to struggle with that, but I finally had to know! Burt said it was up to me because he only wanted a normal, healthy baby, no matter what the sex."

"He's a perfect husband and will make a great father."

"Don't I know it!"

"Your family must be so excited about the first grandchild," Katherine said. She unwrapped a package of diapers that was on the dresser. She put them in the drawer.

"Oh, my, yes. I'm having a hard time keeping Mother from buying out the baby stores." Mary laughed. "Even I know the baby will outgrow all those clothes she bought."

"I was always envious of your big family," Katherine said. "When you included me in many of your activities, it was great." She laughed. "I even had my big brother in Andy."

"Not just a big *brother* anymore," Mary said slyly.

A blush dyed Katherine's cheeks.

"No, he's a man now and interested in Melissa and not as a big brother," Katherine answered.

"Don't you believe it. Melissa will never get him, no matter how hard she tries," Mary insisted. "Andy and she have a business lunch occasionally, but that's all. Seems to me, he's only been seeing you."

Katherine looked at her friend and saw a worried frown.

"What's troubling you? Is it about Andy and me?"

"Heavens, no. I only wish he wouldn't drag his feet."

"Something about the baby you haven't told me?"

"The baby and I are just fine," Mary said. "It's Andy. He's worrying too much—imagining the worst scenarios. I guess he can't forget about Allison and his son."

"That's natural."

"Not the way he's behaving."

"Well, there's nothing you can do about it. When you have a natural and safe delivery, he'll realize he's been wrong."

"At least the baby isn't due until after the opening of the factory. Can't have too much going on at the same time."

"Everything is getting done on schedule, so Andy tells me," Katherine said. "The office is running smoothly because of Melissa. She's doing a great job."

"People do grow up and change. Andy is a good example. With him, it was Allison who made the difference." Mary laughed. "Never discount the power of a woman in a man's life."

"Yes, but there had to be something already there for her to work on," Katherine said in Andy's defense.

Katherine turned away from Mary's speculative stare. She hoped she hadn't revealed her despair. At every turn, she learned Allison was a paragon. She would never measure up to her. And Andy was already successful.

To her surprise, Mary kept on talking about Allison.

"We were all thrilled to go to Andy's wedding. Imagine—my big brother in a tuxedo! Allison wore a lace gown. The church was decorated with white bows and lilies of the valley—her favorite flower." Mary sighed. "At least Andy had three happy years with her. But he's gotten over his loss. I'm glad he's home and happy again."

"Yes, I'm glad he's here," Katherine confessed. It comforted her to hear Mary say Andy's time of grief was over for him.

Mary hugged her. "Good. Let's go to the Sugar Bowl for an ice cream soda for you and a glass of milk for me."

The days in August were unusually chilly. On Thursday afternoon Katherine was alone in the library.

Queenie had crept into her lap, and her purrs rumbled like a freight train. Katherine found her to be a great companion and often talked to her. Katherine laughed at herself.

Queenie had been told about Franklin's proposal, and her dread of the last phone call of the evening.

When the front door opened, Katherine looked up with interest. She smiled at Andy. A sudden shower had soaked his hair and the shoulders of his jacket in the short dash from his office to the door of the library. Katherine's fleeting thought was that there should be a covered walkway between the two buildings. Melissa and Andy were constantly dropping in.

"What brings you here, Andy? Couldn't you wait until the rain stopped?"

"You would have closed by then," he said, shaking a shower of drops from his head.

Katherine laughed. He was like a shaggy dog. And so endearing her heart turned over.

"I only have a minute, but I wanted to ask you something."

"And what might that be?"

"It's time we went to dinner and a movie," Andy said.

"Is that an order, Mr. Stratton?"

"A request. You need a treat after living through this dreary week," he said. "Six-thirty okay to pick you up tonight?"

"Sounds good to me. It's just what I needed." Katherine smiled and kept her seat. She really wanted to run to him and hug him. To have him kiss her and make her spirits soar.

"You've made my day, you know," he said.

"And you've made mine," Katherine answered, her smile lighting up her face like a ray of sunshine and not knowing it wreaked havoc to Andy's frame of mind. She saw Andy suck in a deep breath and saw a startled look come into his eyes. She was puzzled and wondered what he was thinking.

Abruptly, he mumbled, "Bye. I'll see you tonight." With a wave of his hand, he left.

The Wedding Cake

Katherine watched him saunter through the rain to his office building, acting as though the sun was shining.

How like Andy to do the unexpected, and just what she longed for. Happiness brightened her day, chasing away the dark shadows and the pouring rain.

Chapter Eleven

The rain stopped by the time Andy came for her.

"Thought we'd eat at the Rocky Ledge Hotel and then take in the comedy in Bradford," Andy said.

"Don't I get a say?" Katherine asked. When Andy stopped buckling his seat belt, she suppressed a smile.

"What do you want to do, then?" he asked.

"We'll do as you've planned. I'd like some input sometimes."

"I'll remember that the next time. Honest," Andy said with a grin.

It didn't take long to reach the hotel. Inside, the waiter seated them at a table that bordered the wall at the edge of the ledge. A narrow flower box of pink impatiens and white begonias lined the top. A beautiful setting. Then Katherine revised her adjective from

128

plain "beautiful" to "magically romantic." Or it could be if the right words were spoken after warm lips met . . .

During dinner, after a little prodding, Andy told her more about his life in Oregon.

"My Uncle Frank was great. From the start, he saw how important computers were going to be. He got in on the ground floor. He made sure I went to school and also found work for me. Through him, I met Allison. He had known her since she was a little girl. Her death hit him hard. In order to get away from his memories, he took an early retirement and moved to New Mexico. Fortunately, he met a wonderful woman there and is now happily married."

"Always love a happy ending," Katherine said.

She looked at Andy. His smile made the laugh lines around his eyes deepen to make him even more devastatingly handsome. His hand reached across the table to take hers in his. He looked into her eyes, his gaze reaching deep into her heart.

"I want a happy ending in my life too," he said. "With you in it."

Katherine's heart began to race, and she was short of breath. Had she heard correctly? Or was she dreaming?

"This afternoon I realized something important."

"Yes?"

"You mean more to me than just an old friend and my sister's best friend." He tightened the grasp he had of her hand.

Her spirits soared with wondrous joy and happiness.

"Katherine," he whispered, and his voice broke.

They gazed at each other, never knowing the waiter served their dessert and coffee.

Katherine waited for Andy to say the longed-for words. *Please, please,* she prayed silently, *don't let me be mistaken.*

"Katherine, I don't know how to say it." Then his words came out in a rush, "I love you! Where have I been all these years? I've been as blind as a bat."

"Oh, not anymore, I hope," she whispered.

Andy quickly put some bills in the waiter's folder.

"Come," he said, and he led her out of the hotel.

Andy held her hand until they reached the car. His arms enclosed her in a crushing embrace, and his lips took full possession of hers. At first, the kiss was tender and exploring. It became deeper and more demanding as they felt the love flowing between them.

Gasping finally for breath, Katherine leaned back in his arms. Her eyes slowly opened, and she gazed into his eyes.

"Wow," she murmured.

Andy smiled down on her and chuckled. "Let's get out of here," he said and opened the car door. He leaned over and kissed her again.

It took only a few minutes to reach Lookout Point, a rest area overlooking Cherry Valley. In the deep shadow of a big pine tree, Andy pulled Katherine toward him. He held her face between his hands. He kissed her eyes, trailed kisses over her cheeks, and came back to her lips. He gave a shout of joy.

"Yes, yes, yes, I love you," he said. "I love you, my darling Katherine. Please say you love me too."

"Yes, yes, yes, I love you." The words seemed to trip over themselves. She was so happy she could hardly believe it all.

"When did it happen to you?"

Katherine laughed at his question. "Oh, Andy, I've adored you ever since I dreamed I was going to marry you."

"Hey, you dreamed about marrying me?"

"Oh, Andy, don't you remember? I was twelve and you were sixteen. You said you'd wait until I grew up."

Andy pulled her tighter into his arms and groaned, "Darling, I remember now." He laughed. "I called you Half-pint. That's why you gasped when I called you that weeks ago. I didn't keep my promise and even married Allison." He kissed her. "At least, you're all grown up now."

Katherine sighed with contentment. "I'm glad I never gave up on my wedding cake dream. I've had to work hard to hide my feelings for you all these years."

Andy put his finger under her chin and looked into her eyes. "Darling Katherine, will you marry me?"

A surge of joy flooded her. It had finally happened and she was speechless!

"Katherine, will you?" Andy's voice was full of anxiety.

She looked at Andy—her dear, beloved Andy whom she had no doubts she loved with all her heart.

"Yes, of course, I'll marry you, Andrew Stratton."

Much later came the discussion of practical matters.

"What about your ring?"

"No hurry. No, I take that back," Katherine cried. "As soon as possible. I want the world to know I belong to you."

Andy hugged her again. "When will you marry me? I don't want to wait."

"Heavens! I can't think of a date this minute." Katherine's voice held laughter in it. "You've forgotten I've waited a lifetime, and now, you're the one who's in a hurry! After the opening of your factory will be best."

"That's a good idea. Our wedding isn't taking second place in our lives."

Katherine wound her arms around his neck, and she kissed him. Pulling back, she looked into his eyes, laughed and kissed him again. This time, slowly and gently, wanting him to savor the taste of her. She loved hearing his groan of pleasure.

"We'll have a church wedding," Andy said, "or go before a justice of the peace if that's what you want. It doesn't matter to me—only that you marry me."

"I do want a church wedding and a reception. I'll wear Grandmother's gown. It's old-fashioned, but I've always loved it. You'll see it on our wedding day and not before. I guess I'm a little superstitious."

"You'll be the loveliest bride in the world to me no

matter what you wear," he said, words that made her love him even more.

"In the meantime, we'll concentrate on your factory and its opening," Katherine said, suddenly feeling overwhelmed by wedding plans.

Andy nodded his head. He pulled her close, her head pressed against his heart.

"You are my happiness now. The time can't pass fast enough for me," he said.

"Nor for me."

Katherine snuggled closer and raised her lips for the kiss of commitment she had waited a lifetime for.

Chapter Twelve

The next morning Katherine asked Franklin to come to her house before the bank or library opened. She felt she owed it to him to tell him about the engagement personally.

The morning was beautiful, and Katherine served Franklin coffee on the patio. After the usual empty amenities, Katherine got to the point of this early morning meeting.

She put down her coffee cup and took a deep breath.

"You and I have been friends for a long time," she said to him. Franklin smiled and his eyebrows rose in question. It didn't make it easier for her to continue. "I shall always value your friendship and good will."

"Katherine, what are you getting at? What's this morning get-together all about?"

"Andy and I became engaged last night." The words spilled out. "I wanted to be the one to tell you."

The color slowly drained from Franklin's face. He sprang to his feet, his hands doubled into fists.

"No! You're supposed to marry me."

"I'm sorry, Franklin. I'm marrying Andy," she said softly but firmly. "I told you I didn't love you. You chose not to believe me. I don't want to hurt you, but I thought you should be the first to know about the engagement."

She saw Franklin fight for control. He unclenched his hands, took a deep breath and stepped away from her. Slowly color came back into his cheeks. He pushed back his shoulders.

"I wish you every happiness," he said through unsmiling lips. He turned and left.

Her knees weak, Katherine sank into a chair. She felt as though she had hurt a defenseless animal. But she had to do it, and she was glad the deed was done. She hoped that as time went by, Franklin would realize that his pride, more than his heart, had been wounded.

Melissa came to see her during her coffee break. She didn't waste any polite words.

"Well, you finally did it. You've chased after Andy practically all your life. I hope you're not going to be disappointed. Andy isn't the man you think he is. He'll never make you happy or cause your dreams to come true."

With a toss of her head and a tight smile, Melissa left the library.

Katherine shivered. There had been venom in Melissa's speech. Why did she say Andy wouldn't make her happy? What did she know? Or was it just wishful thinking? Katherine realized she didn't know the grown-up Andy. What were his deepest thoughts about . . . well, anything? She hadn't a clue.

She shrugged her shoulders. *So what*, she thought. *I'm completely happy today because Andy loves me. That is all that matters. It'll be wonderful to discover each other in the coming years. Isn't that what married couples do?*

However, in the days that followed, Katherine became aware of a certain reticence in Andy. Unease filled her.

Conversation wasn't the main component of their time together. Andy was very good at kissing her and holding her. When he ran his fingers through her hair and kissed the nape of her neck, she melted. He knew all the right words to express his great love for her.

Andy came over for dinner on Friday night. After they ate, Katherine led him to the couch. She snuggled in his arms, content to have him kiss her for several minutes.

"When we decided to have the wedding on the third Saturday of October, it seemed like we had plenty of time to plan for it," she mused.

"It is a long time away. Much too long for me," Andy turned her face to him and kissed her. She ended the kiss with a little sigh of regret.

"Andy, we really have to make some plans and get

things moving. What do you think of fall colors, like rust, burnt orange, green, and gold for the color schemes for the attendants and the decorations at our wedding?"

Andy looked blankly at her. "You're asking me about colors? You must be kidding. I'm practically color-blind."

"Oh, you," she said and her lips found his. "Then I'll do as I please."

"I think you'd better."

"About the reception—"

"Mother and Mary will be glad to help you." Andy sighed and ran his hand across his eyes. "Sorry, honey, but I'm tired. It's been a tough week, and there's still so much that has to be done before I can open the factory. This wedding is important to me—believe me. It's just that I'd appreciate it if you could handle the details."

Katherine saw how drawn Andy looked. Contrite, she stroked his cheek. "Oh, darling, I'm sorry I haven't been more thoughtful."

"I'll be more cooperative in the future." He pulled her to him and kissed her. "This is what I need and want now."

In the days that followed their engagement, Katherine thought about Andy's other marriage and his first wife. These considerations took on a life of their own and tortured her. She wondered if Andy was comparing her to Allison. She was afraid to bring it up. Andy made no mention of his other life except to say the past had no hold on him. He was only looking forward, with great anticipation, to a life with her.

After several difficult arguments, Katherine finally persuaded Andy that their future home would be in her house. Her mother had given the house to her last Christmas.

"I'll buy the house from you," he said.

"That's ridiculous. I won't accept a penny from you. When we're married, we'll share everything." Katherine was tempted to stamp her foot in frustration. "I'm changing the deed and putting both our names on it."

"No, but—"

"Please, darling. This house is perfect for us."

Andy threw up his hands in defeat.

There were five bedrooms. The room on the corner and next to the master bedroom would be perfect for the nursery.

Katherine had always dreamed of having more than one child. She had been so lonely having no brothers or sisters. The house was big enough for—well, three was a good number! She broached the number to Andy.

"Andy, what do you think of having three children in our family?"

"Three!" His voice rose an octave. "Really, Katherine, don't people start with one?" He took a deep breath. "And, maybe, none at all?"

At that point he reached over to gather her into his arms and kiss her again and again. His last statement was forgotten. But much later, just before she fell asleep, it came to haunt her.

None at all?

Surely he couldn't have meant it. Yet she recalled that Andy never brought up the subject of having a family after they married. She knew it was a big step, but a very natural one to her. Marriage and family went together. That was what life was about. He and Allison must have believed this. So, it would be the same with Katherine and Andy. Of course, she must have misunderstood him.

"Ugh," Mary said the next day as she lowered herself gingerly onto the window seat in the library that overlooked her brother's building. "Katherine, please check and see if I do have the same style and color shoe on each foot? I can't see my feet anymore."

Katherine laughingly did as Mary asked.

"Both the same color and design, Mary dear. Really, you look wonderful. Your pregnancy has made you more beautiful than ever."

Katherine sat down beside her and looked out the window. She couldn't resist her sigh.

"I still make the mistake of looking out, expecting to see the hills and trees. Instead, there's Andy's building," she said ruefully.

"Do you mind it so much?" Mary asked. "It doesn't make you love Andy less because he got your lot?"

"Of course not. I've gotten over any resentment about not getting it. I've rearranged much of the library so that I almost have what I wanted in an addition. It's amazing what one can do when forced to do it."

"I know Andy worries about it."

"Really? He never mentions it to me."

"Andy wouldn't intentionally say or do anything that would make you unhappy. You know that, don't you?"

Katherine nodded her head, but she didn't express any of her doubts. For Andy was making her unhappy, and she didn't want to bring it up. He still wouldn't have a serious talk about having a family early in their marriage. She was trying to be patient by waiting until the factory opened. After that big event, she was determined to talk to him. In the meantime, she held tight to her dream of a family of three children. She didn't care about what sex, but thought it would be perfect to have at least one boy—in the image of Andy, of course.

"Not too much longer for you," she said to Mary. "Everything still okay?"

"The doctor is confident. The baby isn't due until after the factory opening so Andy will have to continue to worry until then."

"Andy's worried? What for? You've told him the results of your tests are excellent."

"Yes, but—"

"I know what you mean. He can be very stubborn about what he believes. Look at the hard time I had until he agreed about the house."

Mary laughed and got up with a groan. "I'd just as soon have this baby early."

"No!" Katherine cried. "Don't say that."

Recalling that Allison's baby had been premature and had not survived, a chill crawled up her spine. Not Mary's baby, never hers.

Mary slapped a hand over her mouth in dismay. "I'm sorry, I shouldn't have said that. Never fear. There's no danger—believe me." She walked to the door. "And I'll be careful to never say such a careless, stupid thing when Andy is around either."

"Good."

After Mary left, Katherine reached for the book someone had returned. The sunshine coming through the window shined on the diamond in her engagement ring. Katherine turned her hand, this way and that way, loving the way it sparkled and glittered. It was as though the fire in the heart of the gem was ignited by the sun. The fantastic skill of diamond cutters to achieve such beauty intrigued Katherine. Andy had chosen a particularly beautiful ring for her. A big diamond in the center with two smaller chips on either side of it. She never tired of looking at it and thinking about what it meant in her life. Such jewelry did speak the language of love, and her jewel spoke of Andy's love for her.

Queenie jumped on the desk and brushed against her cheek.

"Thank you, dear cat," she said. "You make me feel good. You're my daily blessing." She stroked the cat until she purred.

"How silly I am to talk to you, but there's no one else I can tell my troubling thoughts," she said to Queenie. "There's something not quite right in my relationship with the man I love. He's hiding something from me, something important, but what? After the opening of the factory, I'm sure that this will get resolved."

Katherine smiled as she thought about the factory. It was still hard for her to accept that the small village of Pine View had a factory. She was happy that it was behind the office building, almost out of sight from Main Street. She still marveled at the changes Andy made in the business building in order to go along with the Victorian theme. It wasn't hard to love a man like Andy.

Mary was spending Friday evening at Katherine's. She took a sip of the drink Katherine gave her.

"Mmm. This is good. What is it?"

"A special nutritious drink for pregnant ladies. No caffeine or stimulants. Just good stuff. Trust me."

"That I will," Mary said and gave a sigh of contentment. "Everything is working out for us as a family. I'm pregnant after years of longing for a child. Andy has come home," she gave a hearty laugh, "and the office building meets the Victorian mandates. Even the factory will open on time the weekend after Labor Day. And best of all, you and Andy are engaged."

"Yes, I couldn't be any happier," Katherine agreed.

"To top it off, Uncle Frank and his new wife Mattie are going to be here for the family celebration over Labor Day weekend. Did I tell you that even my brothers, Tim and Leo, have leave from the Navy and will be here, also?"

"Couldn't ask for anything better," Katherine said. She thought how terrific it was to have a big family. She was so happy that she and Andy would have children. Each night, before she fell asleep, she even spun stories about their children getting married. Then there would be grandchildren. Oh, life was so good.

"Your mother must be so pleased to have her brother Frank come visit. I don't think I have ever met him," Katherine said.

"You may have years ago, but you and I weren't interested in my relatives at that time. We wanted to play softball and win against my brothers."

"No game this year." Katherine laughed and patted Mary's stomach.

"Sometimes it feels like it when the baby gives me a big kick," Mary chuckled.

"Is everything okay?"

"Right on schedule and not until after the factory opening. That too is a blessing. I'd hate to take away from Andy's triumph."

"Is he still worried? I've noticed him hovering over you a lot."

"That's Andy. He's more worried than my husband, but I'm trying to understand. I guess he's being reminded of the past."

"He doesn't talk about Allison. I know he loved her. Her death had to have broken his heart."

"Yes, but Katherine, that was years ago, and time has healed that wound. Besides, I know he loves you very much. I can't tell you how happy we all are that the two of you are getting married." Mary hugged Katherine. "I can see Andy as a father. He's so great with children, and you've always wanted them. This match must have been made in heaven."

Mary got up from her chair with exaggerated effort and a laugh. "I'll be glad when this baby arrives. I never appreciated being able to bound out of a chair as I did before I became this size."

"When is your Uncle Frank arriving from New Mexico?"

"Tomorrow. Mother wants you to come to dinner at six o'clock. Andy was supposed to tell you."

"He did. I'll be glad to come."

After Mary left Katherine walked back and forth on her patio. The night was warm and the sky was dark with only pinpricks of starlight piercing it. Katherine felt lonely. Andy had gone to Bradford to check on construction supplies. She wouldn't see him tonight. She wanted to be with him all the time. It amazed her that her need for him was so deep and constant. During the years he was away from Pine View she had thought of him, but had never had this hunger for his actual physical presence.

She sure was in love. Madly, completely, and forever. To have Andy love her made life complete. She was so happy to have him now and for the rest of their lives.

After the arrival of Frank and Mattie, the delicious dinner prepared by Andy's mother with Katherine's help, had been a happy affair with much laughter. Tales about past events especially interested Katherine. It made her feel more a part of the family. She looked forward to seeing Tim and Leo who were arriving the next day. Then the family circle would be complete with her in the middle of it. Life couldn't get any better for her.

"Katherine," Frank asked her after dinner, "how about taking me for a walk to see all this construction of Andy's? Mattie and I will have him give us a tour inside tomorrow."

"That's a great idea," Andy said. "It'll be a chance for my two best people to get to know each other."

Frank obviously wanted to talk to her privately. She hoped she'd get answers to some of the questions that had been bothering her.

"I'm happy to meet the woman who fills Andy's heart," Frank Stratton said. "I've been worried about him."

"Oh," was all Katherine could say. Her heart sang for joy at his words. She and Andy's uncle had bonded together from the moment they met. He had the Stratton family blond hair, now laced with gray, a lean build, and blue eyes filled with good humor.

"Andy had it rough, but he now has you." He went on to say, "You both have many years of happiness to share together. I know you'll make him happy because I can see that you love him."

"I've loved him all my life," Katherine said, "but he always thought of me as only his sister's best friend and too young to notice."

"Good thing he finally woke up." Frank's gaze was warm. "You're what he needs. A strong, independent woman who has taken care of herself and her mother—besides being beautiful and desirable."

"You're too kind," Katherine said, a blush tinting her cheeks.

"No, I'm not." He was silent as he looked around the site of the factory. "Let me tell you about Allison. I knew her all her life and loved her like a daughter. I never saw a gentler, more loving person than Allison, but she just wasn't physically strong. I always feared she wasn't long for this world."

"Why do you say that?"

"Allison was small and frail—as if a puff of strong wind would blow her away. Sometimes she made me think she was from another world, visiting us only for a few years. Yet I must say, she could be as stubborn and determined as the next woman. When she decided she wanted a baby, that was it. She wouldn't let the doctor or Andy sway her."

Frank sighed.

"She should have listened. Still, she was the happiest person in the world while she carried Andy's child. Singing all the time and getting things ready for the baby. To the very end, she was a happy woman."

"I'm sorry things went badly for her and Andy."

"I'm only glad she never had to know the baby didn't make it. She made Andy promise to marry again so the baby would have a mother, and he'd be happy again."

"Do you think Andy is comparing me to Allison?" Katherine had to have an answer, no matter what it was.

"Heavens, no! Don't think such foolishness," Frank exclaimed. "Allison is in his past; you are his present and future. Besides, you're so different that he'll never make the mistake of confusing you two."

Katherine was comforted to have Frank take her hands in his and squeeze them.

"Katherine, Andy loves you. Don't doubt it. You'll have a contented and joyful life together with the children you both want. Thanks for showing me the buildings. I'm proud of Andy."

"We all are."

He laughed. "I see Andy coming to get you. I knew he would be looking for you."

Impulsively, Katherine hugged him and kissed him on the cheek.

"Thank you," she said. She felt sure he understood that his words had comforted her and answered her questions. She greeted Andy with a kiss.

"You two must have had a good talk," he said.

"You've got yourself a fine woman, Andy. You'll have to come and visit Mattie and me after you're married. New Mexico is sure different from Oregon. You'll like it."

"We'll look forward to the visit. Right now, I'd like to show Katherine something in the garden," Andy said with a twinkle in his eye. "See you later, Uncle Frank."

After his brothers came, they played the customary softball game. Andy and she had just managed to defeat his two brothers.

"You better hang on to Katherine," Tim told Andy.

"With her on your team, your business will be a success."

"Don't you think I know it? Plan on getting leave the third weekend in October. I want you for my best man." Andy turned to Leo. "You have to be one of the ushers, so that goes for you too."

"Sure thing," they answered.

Katherine and Andy took Frank and Mattie to the airport on Tuesday morning. She hated to wave goodbye. It had been wonderful to be a part of the Stratton family celebration of the end of summer. There was nothing better in this world than to have a big family. And best of all, a big family was what Katherine was going to have.

Chapter Thirteen

The grand opening of the factory the following Friday was an event everyone in the village had looked forward to. After Andy cut the ribbon, one hundred happy employees entered the building. He had wanted Katherine to share the cutting ceremony with him, but she refused.

"Andy, this is your big day. You alone should cut the ribbon," she insisted. "Don't worry, I'll be right there."

Andy cut the ribbon amid the cheers of the crowd.

Andy's executive staff were the tour guides. Small groups of villagers trailed behind them. They were amazed and bewildered to learn how complicated the manufacturing of a tiny chip was. Their eyes became glazed as the guide pointed out the layering process.

However, though the technology was over their heads, they could relate to the need for clean rooms.

These rooms had to be ten thousand times cleaner than a hospital operating room. The factory room couldn't have even one speck of dust per cubic foot. And each person working in an intel cleanroom had to wear special "bunny suits" to protect the chips from human particles such as skin flakes or hairs.

All the visitors laughed as they watched one new employee struggle for nearly thirty minutes to put on one of the suits.

"You look like you're taking a flight on the space shuttle, Mabel," laughed her husband.

"I feel like it, wearing this suit, helmet, and booties," she answered.

"Just think, honey, you have to don this suit every time you leave and come back again."

Everyone joined in her groan.

Hours later, Katherine was ready to go home and kick off her shoes. Open house for the new factory was almost at an end. It had been everything she could have wished for to please Andy. Tomorrow, work would begin in earnest in the spotless and well ventilated rooms of Stratton Computer Company.

Only a few more hours until everyone would be gone.

Katherine looked at Mary and hurried to her side.

"What's wrong?" she asked, not liking what she saw. Mary's face was white and perspiration beaded on her forehead. She panted for air.

The Wedding Cake

Mary gripped Katherine's hand.

"I've got to go to the ER. My pains are getting worse," she gasped out. Another attack of pain gripped her.

"How long has this been going on?"

"About an hour. I didn't want to spoil Andy's day."

Katherine was furious with Mary. She guided her to a seat by the door.

"I'll get Burt."

Two hours later, it was all over.

A caesarean section had had to be performed. Mary and Burt were the proud parents of a beautiful baby boy. Mother and baby were fine, and happiness reigned in the maternity ward.

There had been some minutes of anxiety and worry, but nothing close to a death-defying moment. Katherine thought of it as a normal birth. Andy's reaction was something else.

"See, Andy, everything is fine," she said.

"Now," Andy said with feeling, "but so much could have gone wrong."

"But it didn't. Just rejoice with Mary and Burt."

"I do, naturally," was Andy's reply. He then turned away from her and strode to the end of the hall.

Katherine joined him. He reached over and hugged her.

"I don't want you to ever go through such an ordeal," he said.

"Oh, Andy, you worry too much." She groaned. "Please take me home. I'm exhausted."

It took Katherine a long time to fall asleep. Her thoughts tormented her. Andy's reaction to the birth disturbed her. Not that he showed much outward emotion. His face had been bland, and he was most encouraging to his mother the few times she voiced her concern for Mary. His rigid control of what Katherine thought must be raging inside of him worried her.

Katherine noticed that the family hadn't seen anything amiss in Andy's behavior. Perhaps she herself was reading things into it that weren't there. She hoped she was wrong.

She saw her words didn't comfort him. Now that she thought of it, perhaps she had been too flippant with her reply. What Andy felt was deep and not easily laid aside by a few words from her. He had every reason to be worried about the birth of Mary's baby. His personal tragedy would never be forgotten.

And, frankly, she was concerned about the effect Mary's rush delivery had on Andy. There was something there that Andy wasn't ready to talk about.

To forget her troubling thoughts about her life with Andy, Katherine spent the week doing research on old houses, hidden passageways, and tales of treasure. She concluded the library building was a very ordinary Victorian dwelling.

* * *

The Wedding Cake

On Monday morning Mayor Tyler came into the library. Katherine watched as he turned to face the window next to the office building. He muttered, "Yes, yes, it can be done." He came to the admission desk. "I have great news for you."

"Wonderful." Because the mayor usually sent memos instead of talking to her in person, her curiosity was piqued.

"Andy Stratton has donated the first floor of his office building to the library," he said with a big smile.

Katherine gasped. "I don't understand. Is Andy moving or what? He hasn't told me anything about this."

Resentment simmered in Katherine. How dare Andy spring this surprise on her in this way? Was this the way he was going to be when they married? Making decisions, important or otherwise, without talking it over with her?

Mayor Tyler looked sheepish.

"I'm sorry. Have I jumped the gun? But Andy didn't say this was a secret." He went on hurriedly, "He says he'll use the second floor for his offices. He's always felt badly about cheating you out of your addition. This way, he can change things for the better."

It was a thoughtful and generous gesture by Andy, but Katherine still felt keeping secrets was no way to begin a marriage.

"This is amazing," she said, her wide smile hiding her true feelings from the mayor. "What a wonderful gift to the village. Not only does Andy provide employment for many people, but he'll also feed their souls with knowledge."

Katherine hoped her words didn't sound sarcastic. She meant them sincerely.

"We'll make a walkway to connect the two buildings. It'll be easy to do by using the two windows which face each other," Mayor Tyler said.

"When did Andy decide to do this?"

"Last week. But I didn't know he hadn't told you. He said he was waiting until his architect finished the plans for the walkway." The mayor gave a hearty laugh. "He wanted to be sure it'll be Victorian."

Katherine felt her cheeks getting warm. She was never going to live this down with Andy. She felt a little better to know another reason why Andy hadn't told her right away. Though she didn't like the way he had gone about it, she was delighted with his gift to her.

How happy the villagers were going to be. They had supported her. Reluctantly, they gave in to economic need and voted in favor of Andy. Now, both sides would be satisfied.

The donation of the first floor of his building was an incredible, selfless act on Andy's part. What a man she had fallen in love with! She could hardly wait until she saw him tonight. He had a business meeting in Bradford and wouldn't come back until 7:00.

When Andy walked into her living room that evening, Katherine ran to him and threw her arms around him. She kissed him with all her heart, hoping to satisfy both of their hungers.

"You dear, wonderful man! How can I ever show you how much I love and admire you?" she cried and covered his face with kisses.

Andy laughed and twirled her around in a circle. He kissed her before leading her to the couch.

"So I see you know about getting my first floor. I am happy to do this for you. I've felt guilty about my building from the start. When I realized I had enough office space for twice the amount I needed, I saw what I could do," he said and settled Katherine against him.

"You should have given the library the second floor," Katherine said.

"No. I looked through the window and into the library hoping to get a glimpse of you one day. That's when the plan came to me. We'll make an arched walkway between the two buildings at that point." Andy put his finger under Katherine's chin and said with a soft laugh, "Of course, making sure it's Victorian in design."

"Oh, you," laughed Katherine. "You're never going to let me forget how I demanded you change your design. I had no idea how much it would cost you to change the plans. I was so selfish to ask you to do it my way."

"It all turned out okay, and I actually like it."

"What needs to be done, construction-wise?"

"Not much. Knock out the two windows, widen them, and put a glass, arched roof over the walkway. We can start work in two days," Andy said.

"But you'll have to walk through the library to get to your offices."

"I'm putting stairs and an elevator on the other side of the building." Andy shrugged his shoulders. "No big deal."

Katherine began to realize that Andy was a much richer man than she had thought. He was so nonchalant about what had to be a big expenditure of money.

"Of course I hope you'll use the inside stairs to come and see me during the day," Andy said. "This is a perfect arrangement for us, don't you think?"

Katherine's answer was a long, heartfelt kiss.

"It was a stroke of good luck for Pine View to have Andy Stratton come back," Mrs. Stone said to the other members of the preservation society at lunch. "First, he brings his business here, and then he gives the library its addition."

"Don't forget that we have a wedding to go to. I'm so happy Katherine and Andy are getting married. A match made in heaven if I ever saw one." Nellie brought up the topic that kept them busy until the lunch ended. "What are you going to wear to it?"

Two weeks later the walkway was finished. Katherine cut the ribbon. She threw her arms around Andy and gave him a loud smacking kiss.

"Thank you, darling."

Laughter and clapping broke out.

Katherine, with Andy holding her hand, led the patrons into the building. The bookcases were in place. Soft green carpeting deadened the footsteps. New furniture for the reading areas would be arriving in another week.

Later, Andy and Katherine had their dinner celebration.

"You are truly my knight in shining armor," Katherine said, and she snuggled against his heart. "My dreams have come true. I had begun to lose all faith in them and then, you came back."

Andy kissed her. "What if all your dreams can't come true? Then what, my love? Will you cast me out?"

"Don't be silly. We'll always be able to find a way to work things out because our love is strong enough and big enough for all that life can throw at us."

"I hope you're right. I'm not as optimistic as you."

Katherine looked at Andy, and a chill entered her heart. He was so serious, and there was a note of despair in his remark.

"Let's not borrow trouble," she said. "I think you should kiss me again."

Chapter Fourteen

Since Mary and the baby were home from the hospital, Katherine and Andy had come to visit.

"Isn't he adorable," Katherine cooed. She held the baby in her arms and gazed lovingly at him. She bent down and kissed his soft cheek. Andy's heart flipped over at the sight.

Katherine turned to Andy. "I can hardly wait until we have a baby," she said.

When Andy didn't answer, Katherine became conscious of how tense he had become. She looked up at him. His jaw was clenched, and his skin was pale. Perspiration beaded on his brow.

"Andy, what's wrong?"

"I don't feel well. Sorry to shorten our visit, but do you mind if we leave now?"

"Of course not. Mary will understand. We can come back another time."

She murmured over the baby for a few more minutes and promised to come back when she could stay longer.

Andy was silent on the way back to her house. Katherine waited for him to unlock the door and follow her into the house. She sat down on the couch and drew her feet under her. She tried to relax but couldn't.

"Andy, tell me what's wrong. Don't keep me in suspense."

Andy stood before her and looked down into her eyes. His hands were clenched and his lips pursed. He looked like a man with a tormented soul.

"I don't want you to have a baby. In fact, I don't want you to have any children."

Katherine gasped, fighting to catch her breath. "You can't mean it," she cried.

Andy continued to look at her with no softening in his stance.

"Believe me," he said. "I will never get you pregnant. I don't want you to face death giving birth to my baby."

"Andy! That's ridiculous! Women give birth safely all the time. Even your sister is proof of that."

"Only because they were able to save her by the operation," he said savagely. "Otherwise, you know she and the baby would have died."

"But they didn't die! That's what you have to think about."

Katherine grasped Andy's arm and made him sit

down beside her. She put her arms around him and hugged him tightly. She kissed him again and again.

"Listen to me, Andy," she implored. "You're not responsible for Allison's death. You should not still feel guilty about it."

Andy threw away her encircling arms and stood up.

"You don't know anything about how I feel or why. Believe me when I say that you and I will not have any children after we are married."

Katherine felt as though the world was collapsing around her.

No babies. No children. A childless marriage.

Never!

"You don't mean it!" Katherine cried.

"Yes, I do—every word of it."

"But I've always wanted children. You and everyone else know this." Tears began to roll down her cheeks.

"I can't give them to you." Though these words seemed to be torn out of his heart, he still said, "I won't."

"If that's the way you feel, I'll never marry you, Andrew Stratton! Marriage to a man who believes as you do is no marriage at all." Katherine pulled off her ring and held it out to him, "Here's your ring. Please go."

Andy didn't take the ring. He closed Katherine's fingers around it, keeping it safe in her palm.

"I love you, my darling. I want to marry you and live with you forever." He raised her hand to his lips and kissed it. "I'd give up my life for you, but I can't, I can't take a chance with yours. Please, please, take me, and love me as I am."

160

Katherine's heart went out to him, but she couldn't do what he asked.

"You know I love you. I have always loved you. But to me, love isn't enough. Not in this case. I'd never be happy in a childless marriage. I want your children. I want to hold them in my arms and see them grow up. I have to have them. You don't know what you're asking of me!" Anguish filled Katherine's plea.

"We can work something else out—"

"Don't you dare suggest we'll adopt or become foster parents when we can have children of our own!"

Katherine pulled her hand away and stepped away from him. She couldn't stand this agony any longer.

"Go. Just go, Andy."

"This isn't over, Katherine," Andy said softly.

Katherine turned away from him. She heard his footsteps cross the room and the door close. Only then did the tears flow down her cheeks as her heart shattered into painful bits.

The unthinkable had happened. There would be no marriage for her and Andy.

She cried until she couldn't cry any more. So much had occurred in the blink of an eye. A lifetime of dreams was gone. And what had caused it?

Andy felt guilty about Allison's and his son's death.

For four years this belief had etched itself upon his brain until he couldn't believe otherwise. In Oregon he hadn't had a family support group to help him, to prevent him from solidifying his erroneous guilt. To him, the need for Mary to have an emergency operation to save her life and that of her baby only made him more determined to never put Katherine in such danger.

It didn't matter that to her, his belief was so wrong, and even ridiculous. He believed it, and only he could change it.

Katherine fixed herself a cup of hot chocolate and sipped it slowly.

Though her heart ached for Andy, she ached for herself too. Her lifelong dream of marrying Andy and having children with him was gone. She would never consent to a childless marriage no matter how much she loved Andy. If she physically couldn't have children, she'd accept adopting them. But to just never have a baby when she was able to was impossible for her. A marriage under those conditions would fail.

But she had to admit, being married to Andy was about more than having children. They loved each other and wanted to be together all the time. She had to stop thinking of only herself and her desire to have children. She loved Andy—loved him with all her heart. She would help Andy get over his guilt no matter how long it took.

She had given up too quickly.

She had no idea how to help Andy. Didn't even know how to talk to him. He needed professional help, but she feared he'd never accept the suggestion from her. His self-concept was that of a capable man who solved all his problems by himself.

When the tears started again, she wiped them away resolutely. Crying wouldn't solve anything.

The Wedding Cake

Katherine looked at the ring she still clasped in the palm of her hand. The sparkle from the heart of the diamond leaped up at her.

A diamond is forever.

But not this one.

The library door opened. Mary pushed the stroller to the desk.

"What happened?" she demanded. "It's all Andy's fault, isn't it?"

Katherine's calm demeanor and ready smile hid the ache still in her heart. She hadn't gone back to see Mary or the baby. She left it to Andy to tell his family about the broken engagement. She felt it was his fault, and it was up to him to explain. She wondered what he said—or what he *didn't* say, was more like it. Mary was asking for information.

Katherine bent over the carriage. The baby was awake, and his blue eyes gazed into hers. She caressed his soft pink cheek. The pain in her heart was almost unbearable. She'd never have a precious baby to hold in her arms. At least, not by Andy, the love of her life—if things didn't change.

"He's adorable. You must be in heaven," she said.

Mary beamed. "He is, isn't he? And he's so good. Pick him up and hold him."

Katherine loved the feel of the little body in her arms. Someday—she thrust the wish away. It was so easy to burst into tears, and she wasn't going to do it now.

Though Mary let Katherine go on about Michael and baby-talk to him, she had come for some answers.

"What did Andy do that made you break the engagement?"

Katherine gave the baby a hug and a kiss before she gave him back to Mary. After Mary put him in the stroller, he gave a big yawn and soon fell asleep.

"It was a joint decision," Katherine finally said. "Andy and I disagree on some fundamentals. Love alone isn't enough to sustain a marriage without mutual understanding on everything."

"For heaven's sake, what was so big that you couldn't work it out? He doesn't want you to continue being a librarian?"

"That never came up," Katherine said. So many topics had never been discussed. They truly knew little about each other. "What did Andy tell you?"

"Not a thing, actually," Mary admitted. "He said the engagement was over, and he didn't want to talk about it. Well, I guess it's between the two of you and not my business. I'm really sorry. I've thought you should be together for years."

Katherine looked at her best friend. How she longed to tell her everything as they used to do. Mary would comfort her, and she wanted comforting badly.

"Anytime you need a babysitter, call me," Katherine said.

"I'll take you up on your offer immediately. How about Friday night?"

"What time?"

"Be at my house at seven o'clock."

Friday night Katherine stood in Michael's room watching him sleep with his little fist tucked under his chin. She hung over the crib looking at him for a long time. Finally, with a big sigh, she went to the living room. She checked that the baby monitor was on. She sat on the couch and reached for the remote control. Hopefully, some good sitcoms would hold her attention.

A sudden noise in the hall made Katherine slide to the edge of the couch. Someone had opened the front door and was walking down the hall. Alarm shot through her, and her hand went to her mouth to silence her cry.

Andy came in and seemed to fill the doorway. He started to take off his jacket.

"I'm on time, aren't I?"

"You scared me," she cried. "What are you doing here? You must have the wrong night. I'm babysitting tonight."

"No, I am. Mary asked me." He stopped. "Something tells me my sister is back to her old tricks."

Katherine smiled ruefully. "She's decided we should . . . should . . ."

"Yeah, Katherine, what should we do?"

"Talk?"

Andy crossed the room and sat in the chair facing the couch.

"I miss you, darling. This week has been hell on earth for me," he said.

He looked so miserable Katherine was tempted to say anything to comfort him. But she resisted.

"This is all my fault," Andy confessed. "I knew I loved you almost as soon as I came back. When you loved me back, I was so happy I didn't think about anything else. Then, you kept talking about having a baby, and all my old fears came back. I couldn't get myself to tell you about them."

"You should have," Katherine said. "I felt you were keeping something from me, but you were so busy with the buildings that I didn't insist you talk about it." Katherine shook her head. "The fault isn't all yours, Andy. I guess I was afraid, and so I made all kinds of excuses. Perhaps my intuition told me it wasn't good news."

Andy clasped his hands together. "You have to understand I was responsible for what happened to Allison. After all, I was her husband, and I loved her. I should have protected her in every way." He gave a deep sigh. "Well, I convinced myself that it was going to be okay. When she became pregnant, you should have seen how overjoyed she was! She never regretted her decision. At the end, she was happy she was able to give me a son, her gift to me. She died before Jeffrey. At least for that, I was lucky."

Katherine's heart ached to hear Andy's words and to see the desolation in his eyes. It was as though the years receded, and he was back in that tragic past. He stood up and began to pace.

"I can't live through that again," he said, finality in his voice. He stopped in front of her. "You understand, don't you, darling? I can't get another woman I love pregnant and have her face death."

"But Andy," Katherine protested, "every pregnant woman doesn't die. In fact, very few of them do. Mary, certainly, didn't."

"She could have, very easily," Andy persisted.

"Oh, Andy, you aren't being logical. I want a baby— several of them, in fact—and I'll only marry you if you try to give them to me." Before she could say more about being ready to wait for him to heal himself so they could marry, he stood up.

"Katherine, darling, I can't, I can't!"

Andy cast her an agonized gaze and hurried from the room. She heard the door slam behind him.

Katherine's eyes filled with tears. They ran slowly down her cheeks, and she dabbed at them with her handkerchief. Mary's attempt to patch things up had failed. She had seen how much Andy had suffered and his unshakable feelings of guilt. That he continued to suffer after so many years made it more difficult for him to change.

Though Andy loved her, his love wasn't bigger than his feelings of guilt and fear at this time. But she wouldn't accept this heartbreaking fact without a fight. She understood a little of what power a belief or a dream could have on a person. During most of her life she had believed in a fantasy.

From the very beginning, her wedding cake dream

about Andy marrying her had been only a dream and nothing else, but she had still believed it. He hadn't waited for her to grow up. After he came back, he became her love, making her deliriously happy. And now he wanted to marry her, but under conditions she couldn't accept. Oh, why did life have to be so complicated and impossible?

She had heard of hearts breaking—and it could be true. She felt a physical pain in her chest, as though Andy was squeezing her heart in his fist. But that was only her imagination. She had to stop being melodramatic. She would be facing Mary and Burt soon and didn't want them to see how devastating her brief talk with Andy had been.

When Mary and Burt came home, Mary looked at Katherine and knew her scheme hadn't worked.

"Hi, Katherine," Burt said. "Think I'll go upstairs and check on the baby."

"Do that," Mary said. "I want to talk to Katherine for a few minutes." She stood before Katherine, her hands on her hips.

"What's wrong with you two? What's so difficult that you can't work it out?" she asked.

"We're two stubborn people who won't change," Katherine said. "Guess I'm too determined to have my way."

"You can change—"

"On some issues, yes, but Andy and I have a very basic one over which we disagree. Please understand."

"What is it?" Mary cried. "You're driving me crazy!"

"Mary, I want children and Andy doesn't. Now are you satisfied?"

Mary's mouth dropped open. "But Andy loves children!"

"Someone else's only. He thinks he caused Allison's death because he got her pregnant. Therefore, he's made up his mind he'll never get a woman pregnant and have her die also—especially me."

"That's ridiculous."

"Of course it is, but Andy has had four years of believing this. The tragedy of it is that he never came to terms with Allison's death when he was so far away from a family support group."

Katherine went to the door. Mary put her hand on her arm.

"Do you think—"

"Mary, I can't think anymore. No one can change Andy except Andy himself. You know how stubborn he is under all that easygoing charm."

"I know he loves you," Mary said.

"But it's not enough, at least not now. He's determined to hold on to his guilt." Katherine hugged Mary. "I can only hope he'll listen to reason or something. I love him so much, but I can't marry him unless there are some changes. See you tomorrow."

Chapter Fifteen

On Monday morning Katherine hung up her dripping raincoat on her return from the post office. The weather mirrored her feelings. It had been a fight to keep up her spirits over the weekend. She struggled to look at the bright side of things. There was the possibility that Andy would change soon. If he became very unhappy, he might try to find a more positive outlook on things. However, all her optimistic thoughts had hit rock bottom on this rainy morning.

She shuffled quickly through the basket of mail. Her hands stilled as she recalled the time Andy had come to his mother's birthday party. He had carried her mail basket and decided to build his factory in Pine View. How her hopes had soared, and she thought the wedding cake dream would come true.

If she continued to live in Pine View, she'd see Andy on the street or in the post office all the time. She didn't think she could handle that. So, she decided she would move away. She was the one with mobility; Andy now had permanent roots in his office building and factory. He had promised the villagers he was here to stay.

She shook her head and finished sorting the junk mail from the rest. She picked up one of the other letters. It was from the Library of Congress. *Ah, no doubt a rejection letter*, she thought. She had forgotten about the letters for employment she had sent out in the early summer during another bout of depression. She had given up on Andy at that time also.

If she carried out her wish for a change of location, Washington, D.C. was still her first choice. But there were other places. She wasn't that hard to please. However, her heart seemed to drop in her chest at the thought of leaving Pine View, of leaving her home and a job she loved.

She slid the letter opener across the edge of the envelope. The letter was brief. Katherine's gaze skimmed carelessly over the words. Then she gasped. It wasn't a rejection. It was a request for her to appear for an interview!

We can offer you a position with us.

Katherine read the letter over and over. The Library of Congress. A dream job. A move up the ladder.

Katherine turned slowly, and her gaze swept the downstairs of the Pine View Library. She imagined it to be the Library of Congress main room. Of course, there was no comparison. What a wonderful opportunity for her. And it also came at the right moment. This was her chance to move away and start a new life. However, it wasn't going to be easy to go away. If only she didn't feel she had to do so.

Katherine called and made an appointment for the job interview. This coming Friday at 2:00 P.M. She decided not to tell anyone about it. It could fall through. There would be plenty of time to resign from her position here. Since jobs were scarce in the present day economy, getting a replacement for her job would be no problem.

She called Mary.

"I've decided to go to Washington for a few days. I want to leave Friday morning and come back Sunday afternoon. Will you feed Queenie?"

"Of course. It'll do you good to get away."

The position at the Library of Congress was hers. Katherine agreed to a starting date in two months. During this time she'd have to find a replacement for her job, close up a house, and pack all of her belongings. A very busy time for her, with no time to think about Andy or to be sad.

After the job interview, Katherine spent the rest of the weekend sightseeing. How much more enjoyable it would have been if Andy was with her—to pore over the Declaration of Independence and the Bill of Rights. The security was intense, but she forgot about it just to be able to see the real thing and feel the thrill of living in a free country.

After she got home from Washington, D.C., Katherine went to see Mary.

"I've got wonderful news. I'm going to go to work at the Library of Congress in two months. I went for an interview and I'm hired!" she said to Mary.

"You can't do this," Mary wailed. "That Andy. He's the reason you're leaving, isn't he?"

"No, he's only part of it. I've been thinking of doing this many times. I sent out resumes months ago. Since I never told you, it only seems like a hasty decision."

She had seen Andy only at a distance during the previous week. Today she saw him and Melissa enter the restaurant next door at lunchtime and heard Andy's laugh. Let him be happy with a career woman like Melissa, she thought. Still, it hurt.

"Does Andy know?" Mary asked.

"I haven't spoken to Andy. You're the first person to know. He'll find out soon enough," Katherine said. "Thanks for taking care of Queenie."

After her lunch, Katherine typed her resignation. When she read it over, tears filled her eyes. She had been very content here, and suddenly Washington seemed very big and frightening. Was she going to be happy there? Make friends easily? Everyone she met at the library had been nice to her and welcomed her. Still, nothing could replace Pine View in her heart.

173

She went to the Village Center, where the mayor's office was.

"This will be a surprise, but here is my resignation as village librarian," she said to Mayor Tyler.

"Wait a minute," he said. "What do you mean by handing in your resignation? What have we done to make you unhappy with your job?"

"I've taken a position with the Library of Congress in Washington, D.C. It's a great opportunity for me. I've loved it here, but it's time for me to move on."

"But we can't lose you now. You have all those programs and things going on in the addition. Only you can do them. You've got to reconsider."

It warmed Katherine's heart to know the mayor wanted her to stay.

"I'm sorry to go away. However, I'll be here for two more months, and I can train and help my replacement."

Mayor Tyler walked her to the door. "We'll miss you and I hope you change your mind. You belong here, always."

After she walked onto the porch of the center, Katherine looked through the window. She saw the mayor already on the phone. She smiled. The news of her resignation would spread throughout the village. If his sister hadn't already told him, Andy would learn of her resignation from someone else.

When Andy didn't come into the library during the rest of the day, Katherine was convinced he didn't care she was moving away. All day, she had been besieged by people protesting and asking her to change her mind.

"I think you're mean to even think of leaving us," Mrs. Stone said. "What about your presidency? No one can take your place in the preservation society."

"That's very sweet of you to say so, but Clara will be an excellent president in my place." She gave her a hug. "Pine View will always be my home and I'll come back often."

At 10:30 that night Katherine prepared for bed. She had on her nightgown, her frayed light blue terry bathrobe, and her fuzzy bunny slippers. She was glad the news was out, and the gossip about her resignation would soon die down. Her lips were tired of smiling, and she didn't think she would ever laugh so convincingly again. And underneath it all, with an aching heart she waited for Andy to come. She wanted him to ask her not to leave.

The doorbell rang insistently. Katherine groaned. She didn't want still another protestor to wail at her departure. The bell rang again. She hurried to the door and opened it.

"Andy! I didn't expect you, especially at this hour."

And here I am in an old housecoat and, heavens, my silly bunny slippers!

"I've been out of town and just heard," he said. He came close to her and looked into her eyes. "Is it true you're leaving and going to Washington?"

Katherine turned away from him and started to walk down the hall.

"Come into the kitchen. I was just going to make myself a cup of tea. Will you join me?"

Katherine didn't wait for his answer. She wanted to put distance between them. Andy followed her and took a seat at the table. She saw his lips were a thin line, and a frown creased his forehead. She hardened her heart against him. Who did he think he was to question her actions? She turned away and poured her cup of tea. She held the teapot over another cup.

"No tea for me," he said, his voice harsh. "Just answer me."

"I'm thrilled about going to Washington," Katherine replied. She turned to face Andy and forced her lips to smile. She was tired of acting happy, but she had to do it now. "This is my big opportunity, and I'm taking it."

"I don't want you to go," he said.

"You've joined the crowd, then, because there have been people all day telling me I can't go. This is my life, and I'm pleasing myself."

Katherine sat down opposite Andy and took a sip of her hot tea. She burned her tongue but ignored the pain. It wasn't worse than the pain in her heart. She really had little hope that Andy would suddenly, tonight, say he had changed and wanted only to make her happy.

"I love you, and I want us to get married," Andy pleaded.

"Can I have my baby?" Katherine's abrupt question challenged him.

"No."

Katherine gave a short laugh. Andy wasn't ready to change. "You know the answer then. I'm going to Washington. It will be one of the hardest things I've ever done, but I must go. You can always come to me after you change your mind about having children."

When Andy didn't speak, she got up and went to the back door. "I'd like you to leave now, Andy. We have nothing more to say to each other."

"Katherine—"

"Go, Andy—now."

Katherine hurried out of the kitchen. She heard the back door slam shut, and she thought it was a fitting sound to end their relationship. When she waited to see if he'd come back, she hated herself.

The next week Katherine finished getting the library section in Andy's building in order. Her accomplishments pleased her. She had two enthusiastic aides to assist her.

She conducted interviews for a new librarian. It surprised her to find it wasn't as easy to hire a new librarian as she anticipated. Though the applicants had the educational qualifications, they weren't right for Pine View. Too young, too old, too flippant, too—oh, just not the one.

Andy didn't come to see her, and she didn't run into him at the post office or in the restaurant. She knew he was avoiding her. It hurt so much to just see him. She longed for his touch and his kiss. Her love for him was as deep as ever. She wondered how long it would be before the pain went away.

Mary also didn't come to visit her and this hurt too. Katherine began to look forward to leaving Pine View as soon as possible. Everything was spoiled for her. Her unhappiness was very hard to bear and to keep secret. She was weary of pretending to be happy and having a smile on her face all the time. She spent the long weekend packing until she was so tired that she fell asleep from exhaustion.

At 11:00 on Monday morning, Mary wheeled the baby carriage into the library. Katherine immediately went to admire Michael.

"He gets more beautiful every day," she said. "Look at that smile!"

With no preamble, Mary said, "Andy went to Oregon over the weekend. He came back late last night. He looks terrible. I don't think he ate or slept in all that time."

Katherine took a deep breath and slowly let it out. She had to ground herself and be calm. The thought of Andy suffering was heartrending. And she could only think that the result of his trip probably meant the end of all hope for them. The trip could have solidified his feelings of guilt into concrete. Surely he went to Allison's and Jeffrey's graves—and relived his tragedy. Pain and sorrow must have filled him once more.

Well, it was better to know before she left for Washington that there was no use for her to harbor a smidgen of hope of marrying the man of her lifelong dreams.

Curse her belief in that wedding cake myth! Why did she still hang on to it in her heart?

"I'm sure his business must have been urgent," she said.

"Katherine! You know he didn't go there on business. I only hope he now has the answers to his life. How I wish I had had an inkling of what was really going on inside of him. He's always so cheerful and smiling that I never guessed he was still suffering from losing Allison and his son. He never once indicated this."

"I know what you mean. I'm still in shock about it all. It just shows how little we know the hidden thoughts in a person's mind," Katherine said.

"What about you, Katherine? I always thought you were interested in Andy, but not that you were in love with him. You're a deep one too."

Katherine nodded her head. "I had to work hard not to let you know—especially after Andy didn't wait for me to grow up and married another woman. Then he came back and dated his old sweetheart."

"I wish—"

"Forget it, Mary. I've accepted what's happened. It's for the best—I hope. I'm grateful I found out before we married instead of after. How terrible it would have been then."

"Come and have lunch and play with Michael. I promise not to invite Andy on the same day. I learned my lesson."

Katherine laughed. "Next Tuesday will be good for me."

While Katherine returned books to the shelves, she thought about Andy's trip to Oregon. Would he come and tell her about it, or would he stay away? He kept telling her he loved her, but he didn't come near her. She wanted to be near him all the time because she loved him. Just to look at him was a joy. For him to touch and kiss her was heaven.

Though she often went to the door and watched people walking by, Andy didn't walk past the library to go to his office. She had no chance to even see how he looked.

Her thoughts continually went over her desires. She definitely wanted to conceive and give birth to a baby—a baby she would carry in her womb, feel its kicks of life, and then give birth to. To create a new life with love was not to be rejected for any reason.

But wasn't she being selfish and self-centered? She was only thinking of her desires. She had given little thought to helping Andy. She had been quick to break the engagement. Surely she could give him time. They loved each other. This love she had for him should include patience and compassion. So it might take some time. Oh, Andy had to forgive her. Together they would work things out.

Katherine went out on her patio that evening and looked at the full moon. The world was bathed in its silvery light. The birds had sung their last song, but the crickets were still merry. The beauty of the night soothed Katherine's soul. It was good to know that the world was a wondrous place, and there was order in everything on earth. She didn't know what the future held for her, but tonight, she knew that she and Andy were meant to be together. Nothing was going to keep them apart. She would tell Andy she was willing to wait, no matter how long it took.

As she had done more times than she wished to acknowledge, she looked across the yard toward the Stratton house.

She gasped and ran her hand across her eyes.

Andy was coming through the gate and across the yard to her.

Katherine waited silently for him as he walked swiftly to the patio. He stood in front of her. She saw that Mary's description of him was accurate. He looked tired and haggard. How she wanted to reach out to him and fold him into her arms. To kiss away the tired lines and make him happy once more.

He held out his arms and she went to him.

Andy held her close and kissed her. Kissed her again and again.

"Katherine, my love, my darling, I love you. I can't live without you. Please forgive me for making you unhappy."

Katherine reached up and took his face between her hands. She caressed his cheek, and her lips touched his in a tender kiss.

"Of course. I love you, and nothing is going to keep us apart. Oh, Andy, I've been so selfish. Please forgive me."

Andy looked into her eyes and kissed her again.

"Anything for you," he said. "Hear me out, darling. After you sent me away, I was so miserable. You stole my heart and invaded my thoughts."

Andy paused to place a kiss on Katherine's forehead. His arms tightened around her.

"The thought of you dying in the same way as Allison because of my actions, was too terrible for me to bear. I tried to give you up—for your sake, so you would continue to live. In desperation, I decided to go back to Allison's grave. There I felt I'd be able to straighten out my thoughts." Andy looked into Katherine's eyes. "Was I acting crazy?"

"Of course not! This was where your guilt feelings started."

"I stood by their graves. The sun was shining, and the air was mild. A peaceful silence surrounded me. Without speaking the words out loud, all my troubled thoughts about my guilt poured out of me in a strange conversation with Allison. She helped me, I know she did." Andy's voice was full of conviction. "I could finally see how wrong I had been. Allison would never blame me and would never want me to continue suffering. I recalled how happy she had been to give birth to our son. When she made me promise to remarry, it was to give us both a happy, future life."

Andy picked up Katherine's hand and kissed it.

"I don't know how long I stayed there, but I felt happy and free. And I remembered seeing you holding Mary's baby. You were so beautiful and so perfect as a

182

mother. I knew I wanted a child by you. To have you hold our baby in the same loving way."

Andy's kiss was tender, and, oh, so sweet.

"Ah, my love," Andy continued, "I promise you I'll give you all the children you want if I possibly can. We'll go through it together. I'll be a total wreck, but that's okay," he said. Then he gave a happy chuckle. "But you better marry me first, don't you think?"

Epilogue

A light breeze stirred the last leaves on the willow tree.

Andy couldn't take his eyes off Katherine in her grandmother's bridal gown of satin and lace. After he kissed her for the first time as his wife, he knew his life was now complete.

When they were dancing the first dance, he felt the long row of pearl buttons on the back of the gown. He grinned, thinking about how long it must take to button the dress . . . or to unbutton it. But he kept his thoughts to himself. The dance ended, and Katherine led him to the table on which was a five-tiered wedding cake.

"We'll cut the first piece together," she said. Andy placed his hand over hers, and the silver knife cut a generous triangle of the decorated cake.

Katherine pulled down Andy's head and whispered in his ear, "There will be no cake under my pillow tonight."

"No need for that, Half-pint."